JANE KURTZ

THE FEVERBIRD'S CLAW

GREENWILLOW BOOKS
An Imprint of HarperCollins*Publishers*

The text of this book is set in AGaramond.
Map copyright © 2004 by John Hendrix
Book design by Chad W. Beckerman

Library of Congress Cataloging-in-Publication Data
The feverbird's claw / Jane Kurtz.
p. cm.
"Greenwillow Books."
Summary: On the eve of the day she is to begin temple
service, Moralin of Delagua is kidnapped by the Arkera,
enduring grueling adventures as she tries to escape, and
ultimately learning surprising truths about her own people.
ISBN 0-06-000820-2 (trade).
ISBN 0-06-000821-0 (lib. bdg.)
[1. Fantasy.] I. Title.
PZ7.K9626Su 2004 [Fic]—dc22 2003049258

First Edition 10 9 8 7 6 5 4 3 2 1

 GREENWILLOW BOOKS

TO THE HIGH TEST GIRLS, INCLUDING REBEKAH,
FOR ALL THE FABULOUS BOOK TALKING.

ACKNOWLEDGMENTS

I'm grateful to so many people who helped me shape and reshape this book:

Jane Yolen, and others who read the earliest drafts of this story years ago and encouraged me to not quit too soon.

My writer buddies, who got me back to work on Moralin's great adventure and who continually fortify me with their laughter and passion for books and words. I particularly thank Jo Stanbridge and Nancy Werlin for their smart, bold suggestions.

My Greenwillow editors, especially Rebecca Davis, without whose perceptive, careful reading, lavish use of the word "terrific," and fearless nudging about weak spots this book would be a pale, limping wraith of what it is.

Kathy Isaacs and her class at Edmund Burke School, who were my first young readers and whose comments forced me to rethink a number of important points.

David and Leonard Goering, who cared about such things as lock mechanisms and topography.

My parents, for taking me to a new continent when I was two years old, giving me scary adventures, and inviting me to wonder "where is home, anyway?"

People who do and describe astonishing things including climbing cliffs, handling snakes, and walking on coals.

THE
FEVERBIRD'S
～CLAW～

Chapter
ONE

It was only because Moralin happened to turn her head at the right half instant that she saw her death coming straight at her. The fight had started the same way it always did, with the traditional solemn steps. But even this routine beginning felt precious—since today was the last day of her childhood.

Step to the right, turn to the left, one knee on the mat. As she watched the trainer touch his forehead in a gesture of reverence to the Great Ones, she did the same. She couldn't see his face behind the net, and he couldn't see hers. He would have no reason to imagine she was a girl, a person strictly forbidden inside the fighting yard. But then what made him seem ferocious as they faced each other?

This was a simple fight. Moralin calmed herself as they made their opening moves. Lunge, retreat, arms ready. But she felt small and chilled, as if a wind had whined its way inside the fighting yard and were blowing on the back of her neck.

"Begin," the trainer called. They swung their fighting sticks this way and that. Routine. She'd wanted to feel and see and—yes, even smell—every minute of this fight. Tomorrow everything would be different.

Tomorrow she would wake to the li-li-li of joy cries. She would be stuffed full of food and dancing, and at the end of the festivities she, along with her awa clan, all the other girls of her birth year, would enter their time of temple service. When she came out, she would be a woman and would surely die if she ever looked upon the fighting yard again.

The pain of that thought made her do something she had not done for years: break training.

That was when the trainer made his swing for her head.

Standing in the small changing room, Moralin was suddenly as weak as pale broth, so weak that the stick fell from her hand and clattered on the stone floor. She didn't kneel to pick it up. How could she have forgotten the first rule of staying alive in the fighting yard? Pay attention.

Still, what reason would the trainer have had to go against tradition? Boys were occasionally killed in these simple fights, but only because they had done something rash or stupid.

It's true that no one would blame a trainer who killed a *girl* in the midst of such dire trespass. But every time she entered or departed from the fighting yard, she used Old Tamlin's secret entrance, always moving into the fighting yard hidden in loose tunic and pants, netting that covered her head, and a hooded cloak. Fighters did not want to see the face of someone they might kill in the next hour.

She pushed away clammy fear. Just as important, what had caused her to turn at the exact right moment? Had her grandfather, Old Tamlin, broken the strict rules of the fighting yard and made a slight noise, a sucking in of his breath? Or maybe her skin had known what to do. She remembered a day long ago when she was a little girl sitting beside Old Tamlin, holding one small blistered hand in the other blistered hand.

"I cannot pick up the fighting stick today," she had said, flinching as he looked at her palm. Just the weight of his gaze made it hurt.

He had pointed calmly at the blisters. "Under that skin is new skin. You must keep going until your skin serves you. That way, if training ever fails you, your skin itself will know what to do."

Even as she whimpered, knowing how the new, tender skin would burn, she had obediently picked up the fighting stick. So today had her skin known? She'd made a move she had never practiced, a duck and then a kick so agile that she was able to knock her opponent's stick to the ground before she even knew what she was doing. Miraculous.

Miraculous? She quickly touched her forehead. Beware of blasphemy. Possibly it wasn't her own skin at all that had saved her. Possibly Cora Linga or another of the Great Ones had whispered in her ear.

She wrapped herself in the cloak. What if on this very last time in the fighting yard, she had been killed or mangled? At that thought she broke the second rule of staying alive: Manage your fear.

Fortunately, she was alone. Her legs began to tremble so that she had to kneel and put her head down to touch her knees. But inside the small room no one could see her. No one except the shadow who had silently entered and now bent to pick up the fighting stick.

Shadows had grotesque faces, so as a kindness, they were given white masks that were molded to their faces and could not be taken off. Shadows never spoke.

They knew their tongues could be removed if they ever did.

The sun had turned the temple tapestries to blazing gold by the time Moralin stepped into the great hall for her noon prayers. She wore her velee draped over her shoulders, hood down. Adult women and most girls covered their heads when they left their houses, but she hated how hard it was to see through the eye-holes.

Tomorrow her new home would be here in the secret temple complex. What work would she do? Would the others talk to her? Every time she asked what it would be like, Mother and Grandmother shook their heads and put their fingers to their lips.

Solemnly she lifted her arms to the central sacred tapestry. In her mind she could hear the elders' chants. "The Great Ones showed us this place of good water in the bowl of a valley surrounded by four sacred hills. We carried our children, under a starbright sky. We built this temple, where the Great Ones now live."

She looked directly into the woven eyes of Cora Linga, the Great One she had promised to serve always. "Tell me of the next step on my path," she whispered. "After tomorrow what will my life be?"

She stilled herself to listen. At first no mysteries revealed themselves. But then she was sure she heard something. "If you cannot see beyond the silver threads around you," the voice said, "why twist and thrash about? When caught in a web not of your own making, why assume the spider's poison?"

Moralin touched her forehead gratefully. It was true. She had been tangled in sadness about leaving her family. Caught in dread about living with the other girls. But the spider's web—as one ancient poet called the temple complex—was also a chance for a new and even wonderful life. She hurried outside onto the stone street.

"Hsst!"

Moralin froze and coughed to cover up her fear.

"Come here," someone called softly. Moralin turned and saw three girls from her awa clan huddled by the temple wall. They had never spoken to her before. She was always the strange one, hiding her scarred hands in clenched fists.

"Why even ask her? She wouldn't know." This second voice was tinged with scorn. Only the highborn were allowed to wear silk, and Moralin could see that this girl's clothing was plain, though she did have a delicate belt with glossy black beads woven on golden threads.

"Right, don't ask her." The third girl's voice was a scared whisper. "Don't ask anybody. Forget the idea."

That was Salla, whose grandmother and Moralin's grandmother were weaving partners.

The first girl beckoned. Her fingers were already stained brown with ceremonial dye. "We were discussing whether there was any way to get outside the city wall to gather ripe starfruit. I heard . . ." She glanced quickly around. "I heard that yesterday three or four people actually did it."

Why did they think she might know how to get outside? Because she was one of the few Delagua who had seen over the city wall? She shivered.

"You're not afraid of us, are you?"

Moralin couldn't shake the feeling that the girl was staring at her, even though a bold, direct look would be impossibly rude. "No." She lied calmly, wondering if they had whispered together about what had happened to her when she was small and helpless.

She remembered stooping to reach for a flickering fish in the water that ran in channels beside the street.

"Stop that," her mother had said sharply.

Her grandmother, more gently, had bent to say something, but Moralin had run away, keeping her eyes on the fish's tail as it swished through the water. She wasn't aware of anything else—not sights or sounds or smells—until the stones behind her suddenly rang and clattered with running feet.

She'd squatted, terrified. Rough hands grabbed her from behind. The next thing she could remember was screaming, screaming, as a hand held her by the back of her clothes, dangling her into empty space at the top of the city wall.

She would have tumbled, dived, dropped down down except that Old Tamlin, who was old even then, had somehow saved her. All the rest of that year she cowered in the house, howling in terror when anyone tried to take her outside. That was when Old Tamlin saved her a second time by doing something absolutely forbidden. As if she were his grandson and not a granddaughter, he had started fighting training. "Now," he told the family, "she will never again feel the terrible helpless fear."

"Come on." The first girl folded her brown patterned fingers imploringly. "We'll be stuck inside for years."

"Let's just go home," Salla whimpered.

The girl continued as if Salla hadn't spoken. "I've heard that a few houses have hidden passageways to the outside. In case of siege. If anyone had such a thing, it would be your grandfather." She glanced at Moralin with a coaxing smile.

In the fighting yard, Moralin knew she was strong and graceful and that sometimes people stopped to watch her. What if in her new life she could have something even better than admiration? She pointed to the top of the high city wall. "Meet me at my grandfather's house when the flag flaps with the wind that brings the afternoon rains."

After a long moment the girl laughed, a high, nervous sound. "You'll really do it?"

"Of course I will." Moralin said, now bold. No one was allowed outside the city gates, but the punishment could not be harsh for Old Tamlin's granddaughter. Could it? Anyway, Cora Linga had said she did not need to be afraid.

Salla curled and uncurled her fingers anxiously. "Won't someone see us?"

Better than admiration. What if she could have friendship? "My grandfather will be at the fighting yard. He might leave a shadow at the house—that's all."

The girls nodded. Shadows didn't talk.

Before she even reached her house, Moralin could hear Mother scolding. Someone had tangled threads in the weaving. Or a servant had made a bad bargain at the market. If only Mother would sit and comb her daughter's hair. But the day before a ceremony was too important.

The carved front door swung open. Grandmother stepped out and bent to pull a dead blossom from a flowering moralin bush. When she straightened, purple flowers from a hanging plant cascaded over her head and shoulders like a second velee. Moralin wished she could see Grandmother's face. "What was your temple training like?" she longed to ask. But every girl took a vow not to reveal anything.

So she asked, instead, "Do you know where I can find a basket?"

"Aha." There was a smile in Grandmother's voice. Her smile had once dazzled princes, and it still had power, power to soothe Moralin—and make her nervous. "What would my grandchild who has no love for the back-bending chore want with a basket?"

"It's just an idea I had. I want to get something for Mother . . . and everybody."

For a moment Grandmother simply stood tall and calm. She had probably heard the argument with Mother this morning and Moralin's wail. "But I hate wearing a velee." Mother, with her bone-strong training, rarely raised her own voice, and somehow her calmness made Moralin shout and flail her arms. Even the serenity stone didn't help in those moments.

By the door stood a basketful of moralin flowers—Mother's favorite—waiting for tomorrow's festivities. Mother must have proudly carried a basket just like this for the naming ceremony for her older daughter. Tomorrow she would carry it again to celebrate the start of that daughter's temple service.

Grandmother scooped the flowers out. "Don't go off and leave it somewhere. The pattern is exquisite. One of your mother's most beloved."

"I'll be careful." Moralin hesitated. She could hear Lan in the front room, chanting a rhyme. Lan was gentle and sweet. Sometimes Moralin's fingers itched to pinch her just so she would learn not to be soft. Lan giggled, and Moralin took a step toward the sound.

Then she heard Mother's voice again. Moralin grabbed the basket and ran, yanking at the velee as it tangled around her neck.

Perhaps they wouldn't come. She leaned against a little-used door to Old Tamlin's house and glanced up at the Delagua flag—red cloth, a yellow feverbird with its great wings spread wide, a worm held protectively in its claw.

But when the flag began to flap and the people cleared the streets for the coming of the rain, even Salla was there, fingering the brown and orange handles of her basket. Light-headed with excitement, Moralin hurried them inside and down a dark staircase. Should she ask Cora Linga for help? She flushed, hearing Grandmother's voice in her mind. "Why do you assume the Great Ones' only purpose is to make you happy?"

At the bottom stood a shadow, pale in the yellow tunic his kind wore. He dropped to his knees, head to the floor. "Look up," Moralin ordered. It was her duty as a highborn to check the red dye on his mask that showed he was in the right place. Shadows were like children, needing guidance.

Yes, this one had Old Tamlin's mark, a coiled creeper. She took the oil lamp from his hand, sent him upstairs, and started down the hall. Their secret would rest safely with him. A shadow, happy to curl in the feverbird's protection, would never betray anyone from his master's family.

The door of the small room was locked by a huge wooden bolt carved by ancient craftsmen. If a person knew how to move twelve of the ivory knobs into exactly the right positions, the bolt would slide smoothly. Old Tamlin had made her practice the secret pattern over and over. "Why must I?" she had finally cried out in frustration.

"I shall not live forever." His voice had been more stern than usual. "But perhaps if you understand the city's secrets, the day will come when you will show people what they need to know."

"Me?"

"Perhaps."

There. She stepped into the dark tunnel and looked back at the three ghostly faces, allowing herself a brief smile of triumph. If they were quick, they could return long before Old Tamlin was finished with his fighting yard duties. No one would ever know what she had done.

She put the oil lamp in a little nook where a tinder purse was hanging. Parts of the tunnel were damp and might put out the flame. "Slide your fingertips along the wall as you walk," she told them. In a few minutes the silent, thick blackness made her feel like a fish, swishing silkily through a water channel, or a flower petal, floating. Listening to the slap of their soft footsteps, she was absurdly happy. Even if she had to sit at temple looms day after day weaving tapestries, she and her new friends would whisper and laugh about this adventure.

The tall tunnel was cold. After a few minutes Salla whimpered, and Moralin felt a hand clutch her shoulder. She let it stay, remembering how she had clung to

Old Tamlin the first time he brought her here. Even now the blackness was like an immense animal pressing against her eyes, but she felt comforted by the narrow tunnel, so different from the high places, the up-swoop of her stomach if she even glanced at the top of the city wall.

"You must face your fear and overcome it," Old Tamlin often said, coaxing her to use jutting stones to try climbing a little way up. It was the only thing he had asked her to do that she never could.

Above their heads people were walking along streets. Silently she counted her footsteps until she was sure they must be under the great wall. Finally, she could feel the tunnel floor beneath her feet begin to slant up. Far ahead she could see narrow threads of dim light. The trapdoor.

By the time they all were standing in the natural cave, her blood was singing with the pleasure of the risk. She pointed to the small opening where light filtered through green branches.

The city sprawled like a giant wildcat in a fertile valley sheltered by the four sacred hills. Beyond the hills were uncivilized lands: to the south, the red forest full of savage people and snarling beasts and the yellow-brown sands that sucked all life from travelers; to the east, cliffs and a swift and dangerous river; to the north, the Great Mountains. Old Tamlin had never taken her beyond the cave, but she knew that when they crawled out, they would be on one of the hillsides that overlooked the city.

At the cave mouth she listened. Not a rustle or a whisper. She wriggled through the opening and used her hands and head to part the brush that hid it. When she was all the way out, she stood in bright sunlight beside a gnarled jamara tree.

After she stopped blinking, she saw that ten, maybe twelve men and boys from the nearby villages stood on the slope, where the ground was bright with raindrops and with purple-red starfruit that grew on creeping vines. "Come on," the girl with the belt said, and they all started to run through the wet grass.

Moralin glanced at their baskets swinging in unison. Full of the giddy joy of the hillside and sunshine and the sweet smell of crushed fruit, she laughed with her new friends. A young man bent to pick a starfruit. He straightened, opened his mouth wide, apparently not caring that they were watching, and stuffed the fruit in. It felt good to stare right at a person's face. His open mouth became a cave of redness, and juice ran down his chin.

Without warning his laugh turned into a choking sound. He staggered one step back, pointing at . . . what? For the second time that day Moralin turned her head at just the right half instant to see her death coming straight at her.

CHAPTER TWO

GIANT BIRDS WITH CURVED BLACK BEAKS bounded over the hill's crest. What kind of bird had a human body? Moralin staggered down the hill, stumbling on her dress. Around her, the air exploded with shouting and screams. A whistling sound cut above the other noise. She turned and stretched out her arms to the man who had laughed so joyously, now falling forward. The weight of his body sent her sprawling backward.

Hands. Pulling her out from under the man. She fought them off, but there were more, wrapping the velee roughly over her open mouth to stop the screams. What kind of bird had hands? The creature hoisted her, kicking and twisting, onto its shoulder. The last thing she saw of the hillside was the basket tumbling slowly away.

She expected to fly, but the creature merely ran. The velee wrapped more tightly around her face, blinding her, choking her. She felt a shoulder blade jammed against her ribs, smelled sweat. These were surely no birds. After a while the one carrying her swung her down and forced her to walk. "Mercy," she heard one of the other girls gasp.

Carry us, Moralin wanted to command. Where are your wings?

Behind her, someone began to wail. Come, Moralin cried silently in her mind to the Delagua guards standing just inside the closed gates of the city. Hurry. But by now, with the rains over for the day, the city would be full of street noise. And the gates swung open only to let soldiers in and out. Still, Old Tamlin would soon know she was gone. And then? And then he would come after her. Until then? Pay attention. Manage your fear.

Before long they were surrounded by strange and twisted trees. In temple tapestries Moralin had seen such reddish trunks and thick branches. She looked around. Only the young—three boys, four girls—had been taken. Everyone else must be dead. She saw now that their captors wore bird masks. They carried spears and sticks carved with the writhing bodies of snakes. In her dry throat, her sand breath caught. These had to be Arkera. Age-old enemies of the Delagua.

They walked and then ran and then walked some more. The Arkera warrior men pushed or hit them every time they slowed down, every time someone stumbled. One boy fell and didn't get up. A warrior bent over him, and Moralin called out the beginning of a war chant to block out the thump of the spear, the gasps of death.

The survivors had to walk faster, faster. Darkness opened its wide mouth and swallowed them. After a while the ugly moon rose to glower down with its unblinking eye—white, the color of restless and malevolent spirits. She covered her head the best she could.

They lost their shoes. Their feet bled. "Mercy." The girl with patterned fingers raised them in a pleading gesture. She and her friend with the black and gold belt crouched like baby birds, their weeping mouths helpless and open. A warrior tried to force them up, but they refused. He raised his spear.

"No!" Moralin tried to leap at him, but hands grabbed her, dragging her on.

On and on. Churning with rage, she staggered forward, cowering under the moon's terrible gaze. One of the warriors was carrying Salla as if she were a sack of grain, but no one gave Moralin an arm to cling to. Only four prisoners left. She would have been dead already if she had been weak—if she had spent her childhood hours at the weaving loom and dye pots as her mother wanted. Thanks to Old Tamlin and praise the Great Ones, she was not weak.

When the moon was low in the western sky, they

reached a clearing. A mass of Arkera swarmed out carrying flaming sticks, their naked faces horrible. In the whirlpool of sound and motion, Moralin struggled to stay on her feet. Beside her, one of the boys fell.

She tried to reach out to him, but she was swept along, and in a moment she and the two others were in the middle of a swirling circle. Salla, her dark hair plastered to her face, was weeping. A warrior man, his bird mask fierce, stepped toward her, but a man in a thick cloak made of fern green feathers lifted his hand, and a woman dragged Salla away.

Moralin grabbed the arm of the young boy who stood beside her, but he just whimpered with a look of dazed horror. She saw a smear of blood on one side of his mouth.

Arkera women began to circle. One was chanting with a high, wild sound. Every time she went by, she flicked Moralin across the legs with a whippy stick that stung through Moralin's thin dress. On the third time Moralin waited for her, listening for the voice. An instant before the woman got to her, she reached out, jerked away the stick, and threw it on the ground. The woman howled and jumped toward her.

Moralin heard Old Tamlin giving instructions. She danced a step backward, whispering, "By Cora Linga, may I die fighting," and flipped the woman to the ground.

The circling stopped.

I'm finished, she thought. Now they'll kill me.

The silence lasted five breaths.

The man in the green cloak laughed, a short, crazed burst of sound. Then everyone was laughing. Moralin smelled the crush of bodies, fought the cloth they pulled over her nose. Everything blurred.

Sometime later she felt a pinch and opened her eyes. A scowling face leered at her. Dark paint was spread across the nose and cheeks as if a big winged creature perched there. A hand tried to stuff some food into Moralin's mouth. Moralin spit the food out and curled into a ball.

In the nightmare she was running to her mother. Everything around her was turquoise, exactly the way the sky had looked from the top of the city wall when she was dangling in midair, seeing nothing but sky, feeling terror and the flickity-flick of soft rain against her face. In her nightmare Mother was not smiling and not frowning, but standing just beyond Moralin's outstretched fingers. "Mamita," Moralin called in the dream, even though she wasn't a little girl anymore. "Mamita, wait."

"Chagat!"

Moralin flashed awake. She was sweating, and her bones ached. Her earlobe stung where the ring must have gotten torn out as she struggled. Slowly she opened her eyes to silver-pale dawn.

"Chagat." The warrior poked at her with his snake-stick. The strange word was rock-ugly. He had taken the bird mask off, and she could see his matted hair and glinting eyes. He shook the stick at her as if she might fight. Or cry out.

In the fighting yard she had thought she liked fear, that fine, shimmering tightness when she could feel every muscle singing. But that fear wasn't like this feeling, her breath fuzzy in her throat as though she had swallowed a mouthful of winged insects.

After a moment he walked away, turning once to scowl at her. Moralin eased her breath out in a shaky sigh and scrunched her velee into a kind of pillow, twisting her fingers tenderly into the soft silk cloth. If she ever got home, she'd wear the velee and never complain. "The cloth saves us," Old Tamlin often said to her. "It's the only way."

She closed her eyes, but her mother was gone. The ground was like cold, lumpy bones under her hip, and the red glissim of the trees irritated her even when her eyes were closed. Deep in the woods a feverbird screamed.

She groped in her pocket for the serenity stone she'd carried since her seventh year. In a small home ceremony Grandmother had put it into Moralin's hand, saying, "Someday, my child, anyone who looks at you will see only smoothness."

She found the center, glossy from where her thumb had rubbed it. From Old Tamlin, she had learned that you could be perfectly still even with insects crawling on you. Who would want to look around an Arkera camp anyway?

At home her family would be waking up to the smell of festival foods, to joy cries and the fine harmonies of the chants floating out from the temple. How could she have ever been angry with her mother? If she could just get home, she would never quarrel with anyone again.

The night air was cold. Had anything harmed her while she slept outside under the angry eye of the pale moon? Cautiously she rubbed her aching feet against each other. Her legs were sore, too. Everything hurt. She lifted the serenity stone to her lips and whispered, "I wish I were dead."

Instantly she was afraid. Delagua girls had died yesterday. Wait, Cora Linga, she thought. Don't listen to my foolishness. I didn't mean it. Could Cora Linga hear her? By now Moralin was far away from the temple where the Great Ones lived.

She tried not to think about what might be breathing in the red forest. Grandmother told haunting stories of forest creatures that tore people to pieces hundreds of years ago when the Delagua had roamed this area, living in tents, fighting the Arkera for food and scarce water. That was before the city with its comforting, thick wall. Before a mysterious messenger of the Great Ones gave a Delagua royalborn the secret of making silk cloth, cloth that felt like water rippling in a person's hands, cloth so sumptuous that caravans came from faraway kingdoms to trade for it. People whispered that the thread came from the fuzz of special leaves. Or spiders spun it.

Once the wall was in place, villages sprang up to the west and south of the city like dawn plants after rain. They offered the Delagua food in tribute, grateful for protection provided by the soldiers who patrolled the area enclosed by the four sacred hills. Whenever a caravan from a faraway city drew near, the soldiers placed lengths of cloth outside the gate where the traders, who had traveled for many days, could lay their goods down and retreat. Then the Delagua elders made their decisions whether or not to accept the silent trade.

Moralin hugged her shoulders, longing to be safe inside those gates again, not out here with . . . with beasts. And the moon, that bald, bone-colored murderer.

Where was Salla? There had to be a way to escape. The Arkera might be ferocious, but Moralin had high-born Delagua blood and a Delagua brain on her side.

She lay tense and silent until the morning sun turned the trees scarlet and beetles began to scuttle in the dirt. Then she sat up and looked around the camp.

Here and there people were crawling out of small domes fashioned of animal skin. Nearby a woman dropped twigs into a fire ring, then stooped and blew on the coals until the twigs brighted up. A man thumped softly on a ponga.

The lump beside Moralin stirred. A girl with tangled light hair shook off a coarse blanket and sat up. Moralin looked away politely, waiting for the girl to leave. When she didn't hear any noise, she turned back. The girl stuck a finger toward Moralin's face.

"Stop it!"

In one swift motion, the other girl had an obsidian knife out, pointed menacingly at Moralin's neck. After a moment she lowered it and then stood with a low growl.

Smells of cooking filled the camp. Women were pouring water from clay pots into gourds. They placed hot rocks into the gourds and then dropped in something yellow from pouches they carried on their hips. This morning Moralin would eat, no matter how disgusted she was. You had to eat to stay alive. And you had to be alive to escape.

The thrumming grew louder. The girl walked over and brought back two leaves full of steaming yellow food. Those green flakes were probably bits of sheena peppers, which couldn't be too bad, since they were sold in the marketplace in the city. But the brown spots were probably dirt.

Moralin looked up and saw a funny-eared animal crouching nearby. Its eyes stared hopefully into hers, and it thumped its tail gently on the ground. "Not for you," she told it.

The girl looked at Moralin curiously. Then she squatted and began to scoop the yellow glop from her leaf, using her fingers to shovel it into her mouth. "How uncivilized," Moralin said to the animal. The animal coughed at her with a low *rrut rrut* sound and flapped its tail from side to side. She turned her back. Civilized people never ate in public. Even inside their houses, Delagua highborn women had their own room for eating.

Trying not to let her fingers touch the yellow glop, she tore off some leaf. The food burned her lips and throat as she choked it down. She tossed the leaf to the animal and watched him gobble it.

The other girl laughed. Dark, painted wings covered her nose and cheeks, and she was wearing some kind of dull, rough cloth that wrapped under her arms and ended at her knees. On her right leg was an ugly pink scar in the shape of a half-moon. Feeling her skin crawl, Moralin studied the girl's upper arm, on which she wore an iron band.

Someone would have to practice a long time in the fighting yard to get muscles like that. Her hair had a

reddish glimmer and was streaked with dirt. "Figt."
The girl touched her own chest.

"Figt?" The word felt funny on Moralin's tongue.

The girl thumped herself.

Was it her name? Fig—like the fruit. A loud *t* on
the end, tongue just behind the teeth. "What kind of
name is that?" Moralin asked the crouching animal.

The animal wagged its tail hopefully and barked its
hoarse bark. Its hair, too, was dirty and matted.

By now more men and women were working the
pongas. The camp was hollow with noise. At home the
air would be filled with high, clear singing. People
were streaming out of their houses, moving together.
She should be walking beside Mother and
Grandmother up the steps to the beautiful, shining
temple. She— *Control your thoughts.* "Old Tamlin will
send soldiers after me," she said out loud to the animal.

Its ears moved forward. But it obviously wasn't a pet.
She raised her eyes. Figt was watching her, standing
with folded arms and that scowl. Her painted face
made her look like some fierce forest creature.

CHAPTER THREE

MORALIN PULLED HERSELF TO HER FEET, hobbled a few steps, sat back down, wincing. Figt crouched, watching her, uncomfortably close. Nearby, children were scooping water from clay pots into small leather bags. When a pot was empty, one of the children would run a little way into the forest and call something that sounded like *ho reeahg*. In response, a woman would appear bringing another pot of water.

Two boys rolled small purple gourds onto a hide.

Once the hide was full, they lifted it with sticks onto their shoulders and staggered off, laughing. A little girl trotted after them, wearing nothing except an animal skin hanging around her waist. The girl veered and ran straight toward Moralin.

"Get away." Moralin pulled back.

Figt shouted something, and the girl giggled and turned into the forest calling, "Ho reeahg." She seemed unafraid of the slithering creatures and skulkuks that filled Grandmother's stories of the wild places.

Amazingly, the next water carrier was Salla, looking strange in an Arkera dress. She was limping and clutching the pot with both hands. At home servants carried large clay pots on their heads and hips as if the pots were no heavier than a puff of air.

Moralin stood up and took a few stiff steps. "Hssst." Behind her, she was aware that Figt had scrambled to her feet.

Salla didn't look around. She lowered the pot clumsily, spilling water. "I'm afraid to talk."

"But it's so fortunate I saw you." Moralin hobbled a few steps closer. "The Great Ones don't like it if you ignore good luck when it comes. You must have learned that in the temple."

"I'm not like you." Salla was moving like a small, skittery animal.

"I'm afraid, too."

"No, you're not. I've seen the things you can do."

"Only because Old Tamlin taught me. No one cares if we talk." She glanced curiously at the side of Salla's face, then looked away.

"I'm sure that's not true."

Moralin ignored Figt. "They can't crush me," she said. "You shouldn't let them either. Why are you wearing that dress?"

Salla stiffened. "I wouldn't even be here if it weren't for you."

Moralin felt her face flame. She hadn't asked Salla to come along.

"Anyway," Salla said sadly, "the woman who showed me to carry the water over here has been kind. You saw the warrior men. What do you expect?" She picked up the empty pot and limped away.

"I expect you to remember you're a Delagua." But Moralin said it softly. What *did* she expect from someone like Salla, pampered all her life? This was probably the first time she'd had to sleep anywhere but her own soft bed or wash her hands without a servant there to dry them. "Be strong," she called.

Salla didn't turn around.

As Moralin watched to see which of the houses Salla went to, she smoothed her dress, feeling the softness of the silky Delagua cloth. When the Arkera looked at her, they would remember that she was Delagua—at least until her dress and velee rotted.

All through the day the pongas thrummed. The camp was heavy with sound and with sweet, sharp smells. Moralin sat in the sun and combed her hair with her fingers. Figt copied her. Moralin pretended not to see because she couldn't afford to get angry. Not over anything little. If she calmed her breathing enough, she could look at Figt's silvery hair and eyes without shuddering. Then Figt scooped a handful of red tree grease from a pot and rubbed it into her scalp. Moralin looked away in disgust.

The camp grew so hot she couldn't think. She found some shade and rested her head against a tree. Figt followed. The murmur of people's voices sounded like a weird singing. How terrible not to understand or be able to make herself understood.

What were the chances that anyone would find this camp? The birdmen had moved fast, but they must have left some tracks. And . . . bodies.

She felt her fingernails, sharp against her palms. Figt couldn't watch her every minute. If it pleased the Great Ones, she would slip out of the camp this night. She could find the soldiers and guide them back here to rescue Salla. She relaxed her fingers. Now she would sleep to gather strength and courage for the journey.

When she woke, the red dusk was already fading and there were hundreds of ponga players thrumming *changa, changa, changa* rhythms. The smell of food made the air thick. All around her, people were eating, throwing bones to the ground, where the skinny animals growled and fought over them. From time to time someone screeched a bit of a loud, high song.

Mcralin glanced around. Figt was nowhere.

Was it time? The sky was almost dark. A man threw wood on a fire in the middle of the camp, and people's shadows leaped across the ground. The warriors had approached the camp from the clearing, so she'd move that way. If people noticed, they would think she was only getting food.

She rubbed her sore legs firmly, the way Old Tamlin had taught her. Then she rose. *Shhhh, shhhh.* As she walked, she made the crooning sound of Old Tamlin as he dressed her fighting wounds. *Shhhhh.* You are not afraid. She passed a fire, and someone held out steaming meat. Good. Hard to get far, weak from hunger. She put a piece in her mouth, chewed, and swallowed, even though the spices bit her tongue and made her eyes burn.

Softly. Ignore the pain, and walk steadily, all the

time pretending to watch the fire. She was almost to the ponga players. Be careful. Move silently, as the shadows did. She would find the soldiers. Soon she and Salla would be home. Home with Lan and Grandmother and Old Tamlin and Mamita and—

Flup. She jumped as something cold touched her leg. The nose of the furry animal. A few steps behind the animal was Figt.

Moralin made a great show of throwing the bone to the animal and then dragged herself over to sit on a stump not far from the fire. She felt light-headed with frustration.

As darkness dropped, the pongas sang with a wild thumping, and women began to wail a song of their own. Warriors in their bird masks gathered near the fire, leaping, thrusting their snakesticks. They tossed something from one stick to the next. A woman warrior began to shake her shoulders and trill.

The fire flared, and the thing glinted black and gold in the firelight. A belt. Ah, this was a victory dance. Arkera victory. Delagua defeat.

Why had she eaten the meat? Moralin's arm prickled, and she thought it was a pinching insect, but when she grabbed at the spot, nothing was there. She looked at her feet to steady herself.

The ground seemed to be moving.

It was alive with toads.

She shrank back. But something seemed familiar about the scene. Something . . . Of course. A picture on one of the tapestries in the temple that showed a ceremonial dance. She bent down. One toad did seem bigger than the others and shimmered with a soft glissim.

"Cora Linga," she whispered. With the pongas, how could anyone hear her and how could she hear anything?

Huh. Huh. Someone or something was grunting a kind of throaty chant.

"Cora Linga. Why are you here and not in the temple?"

Low and soft, a liquid voice seemed to say, "Who speaks my Delagua name?"

Moralin crouched, jostling a few of the toads out of the way. "Are you testing me? I thought you were my . . . well . . . my special guardian. You know me."

She peered at the shapes, but she heard no answer. She was faint and floating. A little way off, dancers began to circle as if someone were stirring them with a spoon. Around and around they went, their barbaric song rising and falling like the ripples of a stone-gray river.

She swallowed. Her head swirled with the circling dance. A Great One visiting a dirty Arkera camp? Something in the meat she ate was giving her waking dreams. "Cora Linga," she whispered. "Is this a vision of you? Help me get home."

Huh. Huh. Toad voices croaked in rhythm. "Who," a faint voice seemed to sing, "who, who can escape the spinner's web?"

Moralin heard the sound of her own panting. "I'll die if I stay here. Even a fly caught in a web may escape with the Great One's help."

For a long time she heard nothing but the music and the sound of feet. As the fire dropped down, the camp grew darker and colder. She could no longer see the toads. Her thighs began to ache. There. Was that quavering sound a voice? Cora Linga's voice, low and rumbling?

"Where, where are the sons of the earth? When travelers quake, they alone remain unafraid. He will open your ears, the son of the earth."

"Son of the earth?" She put her fingers on her lips. Had she said those words or just thought them?

"Where, where is the daughter of the sky? Caught on a thread under the ground. Free her and carry her. Beware, beware of her. Use her not, the daughter of the sky."

"What—"

"Where, where is the daughter of the night? Kneeling in the bloodred web. Go to the web when a sword is at your throat. She will save you, daughter of the night."

"Cora Linga . . ."

Huh. Huh. The voice, if it was a voice, began to fade. It seemed as if the fire had died low, and the toads were swaying toward the embers and then away in their solemn dance.

CHAPTER FOUR

SOMETHING WAS TRICKLING DOWN MORALIN'S neck. She groaned and opened her eyes. The animal panted happily and licked her face. "Get out of here," she said fiercely. "How dare you drool on me?"

Figt loomed over her. She said something in Arkera and then reached down and patted the creature's skinny side.

It was morning. Moralin sat up, clenching and unclenching her fists as if readying for a fight.

Someone had covered her with a blanket and let her lie where she fell asleep in the dirt. Smoke from the almost dead fire made her cough. A long gray finger trickled out of the pile of burned logs. The whole camp looked sooty.

She rubbed her forehead. Toads! What had seemed real enough last night was absurd in the morning air. Grandmother had talked of food that gave hallucinations. The lingering taste of the toad dream made her mouth feel sour.

Never mind. She was used to depending on herself. Today she must figure out a plan for getting herself and Salla to safety when the Delagua soldiers descended on the camp. The Arkera would think nothing of running a spear through them rather than let the Delagua take them back.

Figt knelt and rolled her blanket up tightly. She motioned for Moralin to do the same. "What's happening?" Moralin asked.

Figt muttered something impatient and unfriendly.

Moralin pushed the animal out of the way, hardly

bothering to brush the dirt off the blanket. It would only get dirty again. She looked down at her dress. How long did Delagua cloth last when it was worn day and night and never washed?

In her room, shining dresses hung in rows. Her mother might be studying them right now, wondering where her daughter could be. She saw Mother reaching out, pressing her hand tenderly against the soft cloth. Moralin rubbed her own rough blanket as if she could smooth away her mother's sadness.

She had tried to do as well with the weaving as with the fighting moves. The dance of the loom was beautiful, Mother and Grandmother's arms lifting and falling in rhythm, sweeping the bright colors into place. If she ever got back, she would have the patience to sit for hours helping to lift the heddles and bind in the silky warps that floated over the wefts.

Without warning, Figt grabbed one of Moralin's feet and began to rub something oily into it. Grimacing with pain, Moralin tried to pull away, but the other girl gave a menacing hiss. All over the camp, people were working silently and quickly, nudging sleepy children out of the way.

Figt finished the second foot and leaned over for a pair of sandals, saying something that clearly meant "put them on." Moralin obeyed. Then she scrambled up and limped quickly toward Salla's house. Figt followed.

Salla was kneeling, scooping grain into a bag.

"What are you doing?"

"I don't know. What they showed me." Salla's voice was unsteady. "What will happen to us?"

"I think we're getting ready to leave this camp." Moralin made her voice emotionless, hoping Salla wouldn't crumble. "I guess they're getting ready to move everything they've gathered. Food . . . and us."

"I don't want to go." Salla covered her face with her hand and whimpered. "Deep into the red forest? I can't."

Figt pinched Moralin's shoulder and tugged her away. "Be strong," Moralin called.

At least the oily goop on her feet was helping with the pain. She set her face in the fierce expression Old

Tamlin had taught her to use just before a fight. Even if no one rescued them, she could find a way to get them home.

In front of her, a woman pulled down a hump house, folded the skin, and piled it onto a two-handled tray. She whistled. One of the skinny animals loped over and stood so the woman could loop a leather harness around its body.

"I suppose this one pulls our things?" Moralin pointed at the animal that now was trotting after them wherever they went.

Figt moved her lips slowly as if trying to understand how lips might make such strange sounds.

"Actually," Moralin said, "this one does not look smart enough to pull anything."

The animal grinned at her—and drooled.

Only bare, curved sticks were left. Now Moralin understood the stories about Arkera who disappeared as if gulped by a flapping sky fish. Figt gave her a push. Her gestures said, "Pick up the blanket. Tie this pouch and waterskin around your waist."

A sky fish was only one of the strange things that could happen out here in the wilderness. Every Delagua was told from childhood the danger of ever leaving the city walls. "Our ancestors built this huge city," the elders chanted, "to allow us to become strong. We remain safe only within these walls, close to the temple where the Great Ones live. Praise to the Great Ones who gave us the secrets of the cloth."

A man lifted a giant shell to his mouth and blew a low, mournful note.

As Moralin knotted the blanket, waterskin, and pouch around her waist with leather thongs, she remembered the slope in the sunshine just before the Arkera warriors flowed over the top of the hill. She could almost smell the fruit, feel the handle of the basket against her palm. How rock-stupid she had been to underestimate the enemy. She scolded herself in Old Tamlin's stern voice. How could she have been so desperate for friends that she had broken her training? One day of bait had obviously shown the Arkera just where to fish the next day.

A warrior woman walked by and shouted, shaking a snakestick. Figt pulled Moralin into the long line that was forming. So many Arkera and only one of her. She made herself calm and strong. *Cora Linga, speak to me.* Long before the temple was built for the Great Ones to live in, they moved from place to place with the Delagua. Maybe something of their spirits still lingered here.

Speak to me in a way I can understand. The Great Ones usually spoke in riddles. They also planted tests to make sure people were worthy.

Would she be worthy? She looked around. Could she remember this place if she found her way back to it, and did she know for sure which direction to go from here to home? Even the skeletons of the hump houses were gone.

Some warrior women loped by, waving their snakesticks, chanting softly. Moralin shuddered, but they didn't glance at her. Though her legs were stiff and sore, she did her best to match Figt's stride. Block the pain. That's what Old Tamlin would say. She concentrated on the wind stirring the leaves. Make a plan. She focused on Lan, sitting by the fire, holding up her embroidery for Grandmother to see, holding up her face for Grandmother to kiss.

Now they were walking beside fields the Arkera must have cultivated during the little rains. This was something she would recognize if she could get away soon. Beans and gourds had been harvested, leaving twisted vines and leggy stalks. A twig caught in her sandal, and she stooped to pull it out. When she straightened, she almost bumped heads with the person bending toward her, a person who seemed to have been suddenly woven out of the wind that whirled around them making her velee flutter.

"I was sent to speak to you." It was a boy. About her own height. Amazingly, using her language. With an accent, yes, but her own lovely language.

"Who sent you?" Cora Linga, her heart cried triumphantly.

"Up there." He pointed with his chin to the front of the line. He leaned in closer so the wind wouldn't carry his words away. "You can call me Song-maker. They do." He waved his arm in a gesture that said, "All of them."

She couldn't stop gaping. "An Arkera with Delagua words?"

"Me?" He laughed and lifted a flute to his mouth. Blew three haunting notes. "I'm not one of The People. I worked for them this rainy season as a translator when they needed to trade for things. The iron for their spears and knives. Feathers. Beads, if they're to be found. Delicacies like the fruits my people grow." His eyebrows pulled together in a slight frown. "Now that the rains have ended, I was to be allowed to return home, until they ordered me to speak to you."

She gave him several sideways glances. He was dressed in the Arkera way and had two stripes of paint on his cheeks, but his hair was long and pulled back, and his eyes were not that strange Arkera color.

"I've learned to speak both Arkera and Delagua." Pride flickered over his face like sunlight. "Luckily, the two are sister languages."

"What a lie." Moralin spoke with such force that Figt turned around to give her a quick look.

"Not at all." Song-maker played one long, high note. "They descended from the same mother tongue."

She spit.

He grinned at her. "Many words are different by now. The Arkera word for 'old' is *hadde*. But can you guess the Arkera word for 'young'?"

The fields had ended. She looked around trying to find some landmark to memorize.

"*Yon*. Some words are exactly the same. I can't think of one right now." He laughed again. "Such a look you are giving me. Listen for yourself."

Along the line a chant had begun. The boy translated.

Brother forest, sister forest,
Place where we have grown food, found food,
We must leave thee for a time.
Before the dry winds gather.
Before the time of silent stillness,

When all is hushed and dry,

We leave thee singing.

Our blood runs thick with the memories of thy

goodness

until we return.

"Recognize any words?" Song-maker asked.

"No." Moralin spit again. "I heard nothing but babbling."

CHAPTER
FIVE

"THEY TOLD ME TO TELL YOU THEY WOULD not harm you on the journey to . . ." Song-maker used a word Moralin didn't know. "'Deep mother,'" he translated. "But you must not think of escape. The girl there will make sure." He pointed at Figt with his chin.

These trees had trunks as thick as the temple pillars. She studied one, wondering if it was as smooth as it looked. He was wrong. She would escape.

Figt bent down and said something to the panting

animal. A woman replied sharply. "What is she saying?" Moralin asked. Maybe she could use the boy to learn of Arkera weakness.

He translated. "This one talks to a beast. Not even a good beast, not even a carrying beast, but foolish like the first beast."

A rock was flung toward the beastie. It yelped and ran off among the trees. Figt sucked in her breath but said nothing.

Somewhere behind them a child whimpered. Moralin heard the mother's quick hushing. People glanced around with frightened eyes.

Why? Did the boy know?

A woman with a crinkled face spoke loudly. "'Here is my story,'" Song-maker translated.

People up and down the line echoed "story . . . story." Reluctantly Moralin recognized the word.

The boy tipped his head to listen. Whenever the woman paused, he quickly filled in for Moralin.

"When the world was young, Mama Koy, ancestor of all the tree spirits, sent word to the animals that a new creature had come to the forest, clever but often unwise. Mama Koy said, 'Because of thy love for me, give thy gifts to help the new one.' Obediently the animals came. The one-who-buzzes brought a drop of shining sweetness. The one-who-hops gave soft fur for healing when the new one fell in the fire and was burned. Each animal had its gift. Best of all, the one-who-slithers offered the twelve medicines. To him, Mama Koy said fondly, 'Oh, most generous one, and may the new one always revere thee because of thy gift.'"

Song-maker had a gift for mimicry. He hopped and buzzed so perfectly that Moralin almost smiled.

"Mama Koy stopped. 'But one of the animals under the sun is not here.' All the other animals looked around. They saw the one-who-flies and the one-who-swims. They saw the one-who-burrows and the one-who-bleats. A whisper rippled around the circle, growing into a rushing wind.

"Black-beak-who-soars-on-swift-wings flew swiftly off and returned. 'Oh, just and merciful Mama Koy,' he cried, wheeling above their heads, 'I found this one-who-barks. He was too busy to bring a gift because he was foolishly chasing his tail.'"

The woman finished. Song-maker played a mournful flute sound. "Thus Mama Koy ordered that since the one-who-barks did not give his gift obediently, he must work hard all the days of his life and find his own food so as not to take food from the mouths of the children."

A man spoke in a low voice. Song-maker translated. "I have heard that this one-who-barks can steal the skin of any animal and run about the forest at night."

From their fearful murmurs Moralin could see the others agreed.

That night they slept where they dropped. Moralin, huddled under her blanket, dreamed of a swirling mist with a strange shape looming. She was about to recognize the shape when Figt jostled her awake, rubbing the oils onto her burning feet.

Could she get information from the boy? Was there any way to do it without revealing that her intention was escape? She winced away from Figt's fingers. If he did guess, would he tell the elders?

For a while as they walked, she did not see him. When she heard the haunting notes, she was filled with relief. He ran up, gave her an elaborate bow, and fell in beside her. Figt walked in front of them, muttering. "What is she saying?" Moralin asked.

Song-maker didn't answer.

Moralin studied him furtively. She had to make her move soon. Had he ever seen her city? If he had, he would understand. What was Mother doing right now? Watching the pots as the servants stirred shining threads in the bubbling dye and shadows crept close to the dangerous fires to put on more wood?

She looked around at the reddish trees, brown brush, and brown clothes and longed for sky-turquoise, honey-gold, fire-orange, all the colors of Delagua cloth. No wonder other people craved it; no wonder the temple elders worked hard to keep hold of the secrets of making it. She was ashamed that she had not seen how valuable it was. Now she couldn't imagine that she had not wanted to learn all the important things a Delagua woman needed to know about cloth. When she got back, how much better she would do.

"How did you reach the Arkera?" she asked.

"On my own feet of course." He stretched proudly. "I am almost a man. My people are those who walk bravely from one corner of the flat earth to the other."

"My people are those who stand bravely and defend their city." Moralin gave him a glance of scorn. "And you are no more man than I am woman."

He raised the flute to his lips and played a tune so sad she felt the scorn melt. After a while he said, "At first I was a little frightened to walk alone. When I return home—if they let me return—it will be easier."

The chanting began again. If he knew how to walk away from this place, she must capture his trust. "I've been thinking about what you told me," Moralin said. "Let me try again to hear the words."

The boy looked pleased.

Brother, sister, small stream,
Place where we have taken water, taken clay,

We greet thee.

On our way to deep mother,

We ask for thy cooling water.

We ask thee thanking.

We ask thee singing.

For the sake of Mama Koy.

People stooped to fill waterskins. As Moralin waited for hers to fill, she tried to memorize the look of the gnarled roots of a tree that clung to the opposite bank. Figt gave her a shove.

All morning they traveled. This was a land cut with streambeds, and as they climbed up and down, Moralin felt her muscles cramping. She hoped someone was carrying Salla. The boy stumbled and caught his balance. "I trip." He grinned at her. "Thee trips, you trip, he trips, she trips, we trip, they trip." He repeated the words in Arkera. "You try it."

"Why both 'thee' and 'you?'"

"Keep to 'thee.' It's more polite." He said something

else. "I tripped," he translated. "Hear the difference?"

Cautiously she tried the Arkera word. He corrected her. She turned her head to listen better, caught her foot on a root, and had to run a few steps to smooth her stride and her dignity.

"She trips." He laughed. He bent and scooped up something. A little green creeper, leaf bright, surely a distant cousin to the ugly snakes on the Arkera sticks. "It does not trip. No legs."

She surprised herself by laughing. He held it out, but as she reached for it, a shout startled her. The creeper dropped between them and whisked away into the grass. Three warriors trotted by, their heads covered again with the bird masks.

"Ferocious, aren't they?" Song-maker shuddered elaborately, perhaps as a joke, perhaps seriously. "Once these black-beak people forced us to work for them as part of our tribute. More recently they've begun trading with my people instead, so they're supposed to give me salt in exchange for my translating." He paused. "Even so, I half expect to feel a spear sliding between my shoulder blades as I leave. Now that I know some of their secrets." His face crinkled into a wry grin. "It would save them some salt."

Moralin chewed on her thumbnail remembering baby bird faces looking helplessly up. She bit her thumb to stop the horror of her thoughts. "Why are they wearing the masks again?"

It was smooth enough here for Song-maker to walk beside her. He studied the soot-gray sky. "I suppose the masks give them some kind of power or protection. I don't know. Guests watch their conversation topics. I'm to be out of here soon. I'd like it to be alive."

This was the opportunity. Moralin focused on the back of Figt's head and made her voice casual. "Have you ever wanted to see the Delagua city?"

He looked at her, and she was surprised to see in his amused expression that she had not fooled him. "Oho. In the feverbird's claw. The only place even worse than in the grip of the black-beak people."

She could feel indignation flash in her. *Calm.* She needed him.

"What your people do to prisoners," he went on. "Now that's the stuff of nightmares."

"And I suppose *your* people—"

"Look." She saw they were approaching a huge field. Warriors were already moving through the tall grasses, sweeping with their sticks. In the confusion, the beastie came slinking up to stand by Figt, who leaned down to whisper something in its ear. "Actually—" Song-maker said.

He was interrupted by a woman's voice speaking loudly to a group of children. "What is she saying?" Moralin asked.

"That the helicht grows here," Song-maker said. "Once she found a plant so big that even a warrior hurt near to death could place the oils of the plant on the wound and be healed. She says, 'Look hard, oh, my children, and do not forget to thank the helicht plant before taking its flower.'"

The old woman's face became grave, and her voice dropped. "Take care not to pull up any roots," Song-maker translated, "lest earth spirits get pulled into the air, where they will shrivel and become angry."

The children began to fan out, pushing the grass aside. Moralin lifted the hem of her dress and took a cautious step. "Skulkuks?" she asked. Even a small one of those fierce and biting lizard beings could attack people's ankles and cripple them.

During the deep dry time, when dust whirlwinds danced in the streets, Delagua women stayed inside their cool houses, weaving. Her grandmother would weave words along with her threads, terrifying stories of the red forest and the creatures living there. As a child Moralin had asked again and again for the stories of giant skulkuks, perhaps mutated by the red trees, huge flying beasts that could sweep down without warning, only one water-rippling cry. The stories gave her nightmares, but the next day she would ask to hear them again.

She saw that Figt was already deep in the grasses. Be careful, lest a mere story leave her hollow and quavering. She waded in.

"Wait," Song-maker called, but she didn't dare. Oils

like those Figt kept putting on her feet would be important for the journey home. "Skulkuk," he shouted after her. "That's a word the same in both languages."

When they were near the middle of the field, Figt dropped to her knees. Moralin saw a plant with a spike topped by a sinister white flower. Figt bowed slightly to the plant or perhaps to Mama Koy. With her shiny knife, she carefully began to cut. Moralin was filled with envy. The moon color of the flower made her uneasy, but she had to have one.

Just then the mournful note of the shell moaned. Obediently people began to move toward the sound. Moralin sighed. She took a step and then leaped back from whatever rustled in the grass almost under her foot.

As she fell, a gray bird whooshed up toward her face and into the air, its wings flapping as wildly as her heart. The grass broke her fall. By her hand she saw a tiny helicht plant. "Cora Linga," she whispered. "Was this bird your messenger?"

Urgently she tugged on the flower. The whole plant slid out of the ground. "Earth spirits," the old woman had said. Forget that. Moralin's fingers trembled with the haste of getting the plant into her pouch before Figt saw what she had seen, a brilliant blue bead tangled in the small roots.

As she crossed the field behind Figt, her thoughts leaped, each one shiny with possibilities. It was as if she were living in one of Grandmother's stories. Song-maker. He must be the son of the earth. "My people walk bravely," he had told her, and he had surely opened her ears. Now here was this bead, like a blue bit of sky just waiting to be freed and carried. Could Cora Linga send her messengers even here? Hope burned her throat, making her hold her breath. She would do it: trust the boy and ask him directly for help.

But Song-maker seemed to have disappeared. While she walked and waited for him to find her again, she thought about what she would say. She must find the perfect tone.

Gradually she noticed that people were whispering

to one another. Their voices sounded dire and urgent. The trees were too close for her to see the sun, so she didn't even know in what direction they were moving. Once or twice she took a cautious step or two to the left or right. Each time Figt whistled, and warriors were beside her in a flash.

Where was Song-maker? Impatient and cross, she glanced around.

They came to a slope where the trees thinned. As people found their way down, they slipped on the rocks. Moralin paused. Figt stopped, too, staring at her with hostile eyes. Moralin ignored the other girl, studying the clumps of people for Song-maker.

How many were spread out on the slope below her? Two hundred? Three hundred? More Arkera trickled past. "Wait," he had said, but she had been in too much of a hurry. Had he been trying to say good-bye?

Frantic now, she searched the whole area again. The elders must have decided it was time for him to leave. Alive? "I half expect I'll feel a spear sliding between my shoulder blades as I leave," he'd said. She shuddered.

Figt spoke a word of rough command, and Moralin took a few stumbling steps.

Far below, those in the lead had reached jagged stumps that pointed at the sky. The elders raised their snakesticks, and the wave of people moving toward them stopped as if a river had abruptly dried up. For a moment the air was still and dry as dust. An animal howled.

Every other animal on the slope wailed in answer. Figt flung herself toward the beastie. A child screamed. At that moment something leaped into the sky from behind the stumps.

A wild shriek shivered the air, and the world exploded with sound and fear. *Run.* Anywhere. Away from the glimpse of wings and clawed feet and webbed red skin hung on delicate bones.

The smell of rotting meat choked Moralin. She dashed down and to one side, tripping, falling, hauling herself to her feet, running again. Thick brush grabbed her ankles. She turned even more downhill, scrabbling and slipping toward the trees that would give some cover. Her breath was knife-sharp in her chest. Her eyes blurred with tears.

A rock blocked her way. She didn't hesitate but scrambled over it. Now she was sliding and then rolling into some kind of ravine. A bush at the bottom broke her fall. A huge tree lay flat on the ground ahead of her.

The air was hazy with smoke. Somewhere behind her, the beastie began its low, hoarse barking, frantic this time. The stink grew more powerful, filling Moralin's head.

"Pay attention," Old Tamlin's voice urged her. The barking turned into a yelp of terrible pain. On hands and knees, Moralin lunged toward the fallen tree. One end was open. She wiggled backward into the hollow log, then reached out and grabbed as much brush as she could reach, pulling it around the opening. Carefully she flattened herself.

After her breath quieted, she could hear muffled shouting and snarls. The skulkuk must be attacking. Long ago in the Delagua city it was the fashion for highborns to keep miniature skulkuks chained in their houses. Grandmother talked disapprovingly of the danger and more than once showed Moralin that one of the old servants had a purple scar on her ankle from a skulkuk bite. When the servant was only a child, she'd let fascinated curiosity draw her too close. Grandmother's mother had saved her life, putting hot cloths on her ankle and ginger on her forehead to soak out the poisons and nightmares.

Shhhh, shhhhh. Moralin pressed her mouth closed to keep the moan of fear inside. What she had seen was a giant, monstrous version of those miniature beasts. She rested her head against moss, breathing in the smells of earth and old sap. *Calm.* Her enemies would be busy for a while. No one would have time to think of an escaped prisoner.

"Thank you, Cora Linga," she breathed again and again. She must still be on land where the Delagua had once made their camps. No matter what other horrors were out there, Cora Linga's messengers would help her make her way.

CHAPTER
SIX

THE INSIDE OF THE LOG WASN'T DAMP, AS
Moralin had expected, and Old Tamlin had trained her
to lie still without twitching even when she was terrified. Finally the sounds drifting from the outside
world made her think the skulkuk must be growing
weaker. She could hear the shouts dropping away.

Shivering with joy, she imagined herself already back
home, running over the stones to her house. She could
clearly see Grandmother and Mother standing by the

moralin bush, hugging each other sorrowfully. Now they were looking up. They spotted her and began to cry out with excitement.

She pulled her thoughts back, groping to feel inside the pouch. Not as much food as she would have liked, but she would survive somehow, even if she had to eat bugs. As if it had heard her thoughts, some tiny thing scuttled across her hand. Careful to make no noise, Moralin flicked it off.

"Brains and courage have given the noble Delagua many an advantage against an enemy," Old Tamlin used to say. He had taught her that if she could be patient enough to wait and then bold enough when the moment came, anything was possible. Old Tamlin knew all about weapons and how to use them, but he said over and over that more important than weapons was a disciplined mind.

Using her fingers as eyes, she found what she wanted. Though the inside of the log was dark, the bead's beauty glistened in her mind. Such a sumptuous blue would tempt many, making the bead useful for trade. But Cora Linga had said, "Use her not, the daughter of the sky." Moralin put it into her pocket, and drew out the serenity stone. "I told you I would escape," she said, mouthing the words. She'd find a friendly village. Maybe she wouldn't even need Cora Linga's help.

"Be careful." The voice in her thoughts was so real she could almost believe the stone had spoken. "Don't say anything rash against the Great Ones."

Moralin touched her forehead gratefully and felt, against the back of her hand, the brush of something sticky that clung to her fingers: a spiderweb. Cora Linga had said "Go to the web." Now all three pieces of her riddle had fallen into place, and Moralin was saved.

The elders would be interested to hear that Cora Linga's power still spread so far from the temple. Moralin would give them the blue bead so she would never be tempted to use it. As her time of service began, they would already know her to be someone who had proved herself worthy.

She imagined herself bowing before the tapestry. Her muscles twitched with the longing to burst out of the log and just to run, putting this place far behind. Better not trying to travel until the Arkera were farther away from her. Figt wouldn't be able to think about anything but the beastie for a while. It would be a nasty thing for any small animal to get mixed up with the claws of a skulkuk.

Song-maker had shown her this weakness in Figt. Warm gratitude spread in her chest. If the Arkera elders had simply told him it was time to go, if the warriors had spared him from their spears, maybe she could catch up. She smiled. He could show her how to walk from one corner of the flat earth to the other.

Slowly she relaxed into the cradle of the giant log. Many times, according to Old Tamlin's stories, the Delagua were so badly outnumbered by the fierce and bloody Arkera they thought their enemies must be as numerous as strawhoppers, yet they still managed to win. Now she, too, had gotten away.

Ruuuch. Ruuch. Moralin stiffened.

Something was rooting through the leaves outside the log. She put her sticky hand to her mouth, feeling hot breath on her fingers.

The rooting became louder, and she thought she could hear *waa-waa-waa* breathing. Something snorted and bumped against the log. Cora Linga, she prayed. Don't let me get this far only to be torn apart by one of the monsters from Grandmother's stories.

Just then whatever it was gave a loud snort and whuffled off, its noises growing fainter and then dying away completely. Praise the Great Ones, she was not to be meat for some monster's belly.

It took all her training to make her breathing steady again. Soon she was deep inside herself. In her mind she soared through the air, practicing her leaps and spins. Old Tamlin was laughing, cheering her on.

"Brave girl," Old Tamlin was shouting to her. "I knew you would get away."

What was that? Footsteps. Small, light patters and heavier steps following.

A soft whimper trickled out before she could stop it.

Cora Linga. Save me once again. Maybe Cora Linga would send a fog to cover the log and keep her safe from prying eyes. Maybe smoke still hung heavy from the skulkuk's firesome breath.

Something scratched at the brush in front of the log. And then a voice, a familiar voice, began to shout.

CHAPTER

SEVEN

HANDS GRABBED HER AND PULLED ON ANY-thing they caught hold of—neck, shoulders, hair. She swallowed the pain and squirmed deeper, but the hands were too strong. She was outside the log. Hands seized her legs and arms and hoisted her into the air. Someone yanked the pouch from her waist, the serenity stone from her hand, the velee from her shoulders. She kicked and bit, but the hands just tightened. As she twisted, she caught one glimpse of

Figt before someone pulled a rough blanket over her face.

All that day she was carried, wrapped in the blanket, on the back of first one warrior and then another. She could barely make out muffled voices. It was like being in a great cocoon. For a while, sick with suffocation, she clung to the idea that when they unwrapped her, Cora Linga would have allowed her to sprout great wings, and she would flap off into the turquoise sky, looking down at their startled, upturned faces.

But when they took the blanket off, she only wobbled two steps on stiff legs before a warrior man grunted and unwrapped a leather thong from his waist. He tied her wrists together and then bound her to a small tree. She slumped to the ground. All around, people were eating, but no one brought her anything. Her pouch was gone. The velee was gone. So was the serenity stone.

For the first time she felt despair. Old Tamlin said, "May your eyes show nothing when the enemy is fierce before your face." But even if Old Tamlin raised a whole army of soldiers, they would never dare come this far from the temple and the protection of the Great Ones. She was hungry and sore and cold. She didn't even have an ugly Arkera blanket to keep the moon away.

How had she gotten it all so wrong? Maybe everything—the boy, the bead, the web—was just chance, after all, and not from Cora Linga. Or maybe she had indeed angered the earth spirits, in a place where they were stronger than the Great Ones. Either way, she was doomed.

After a long time a warrior woman stepped out of the shadows, held out an ugly dress, and motioned for her to put it on. "No." Moralin shook her head, hoping her meaning was clear. "No, I won't wear any Arkera cloth." If only Song-maker were here to translate.

As an answer, the woman reached down and grabbed Moralin's shoulders and lifted her to her feet. Two other women walked over. It was clear she would have no choice, and if they took her Delagua dress, she would lose the bead in her pocket. She held out her hand, palm up. "All right." She pointed at the blanket tied to one woman's waist and motioned for them to hold it up, give her privacy. They laughed, but while they were distracted, she curled her fingers around the bead.

The skin dress was scratchy-rough, and it smelled faintly of tree bark. "Can I have my pouch?" she asked.

"Poouuch?" one of the women mimicked. The others laughed. Moralin pointed, and they knotted one of the small bags around her waist.

Her wrists were tied together, and she was fastened to the tree again. A woman carried her dress away. "Don't," Moralin shouted, but the woman tossed it into the fire. The cloth flared orange and purple, then shriveled to a black lump. Moralin bit the inside of her lip so hard she tasted blood.

After they left her alone, she peeked at the sky. At least the moon's eye was starting to close. Old Tamlin, who had traveled outside the walls in his youth, said soldiers found their way by knowing the positions of the star animals that crouched in the sky. She knew only the bright spider star of the south in the feverbird constellation.

All chance of memorizing landmarks was gone. What would happen now? The boy had said they wanted her unharmed, no doubt to be a prisoner sacrifice. She took a deep, shaky breath. Old Tamlin said the way of a fighter was not to court death but also not to be afraid if death came seeking, calling your name.

If she ever saw Figt again, rage would make her strong enough to tear the other girl to bits. And Figt's beastie, too. Had he been the one to smell her out? But now she was with only a small group. Either the skulkuk had killed hundreds of Arkera or the big group had split into smaller traveling bands.

When the camp quieted, she twisted and turned, then tried pulling and yanking. No, she was as helpless as any animal about to be slaughtered. Finally she simply huddled against the tree, trembling. She slept a little and woke to feel the tree burning her skin.

By first light the camp was already in a hurry. A warrior woman untied Moralin and knotted the other end of the thong around her own wrist.

"Can I have something to eat?"

The woman made a shrug of nonunderstanding and gave a tug. Moralin made the motions to show what she wanted. In answer, the woman held out a piece of the black bread. "*Gada.*"

Moralin took stiff steps. She'd say no dirty Arkera word for "bread."

"*Gada,*" the woman said again.

"No."

The woman put the bread in her pouch.

For the next two days they walked deep into the red forest, where the trees grew huge and close and hummed so loudly that Moralin could not even hear the breathing of the people beside her. Her feet had gone from burning, pinching pain to numbness. Her heart, too, numbed.

Every day farther away from the Delagua city and temple made it more impossible that she would ever get back. She stared ahead with stone eyes and made no response to anything.

What would happen if she died out here? At home when someone died, that person was left alone in a closed room to which the Great Ones sent their messengers for judgment and pity. Would the messengers somehow find her? If they did, she could at least go to judgment having died a worthy death as a noble Delagua sacrifice.

The trees dwindled until she could sometimes glimpse a faint purple line of mountains to the east. Smaller pockets of people camped together at night, calling out in high chants or with pongas to other groups nearby. Moralin learned to match her step to the woman she was bound to and look at bare faces without flinching. She learned to sleep sitting up, tied to a tree, her head covered with a blanket because of the moon. She learned to say *gada* for the black bread, her voice sullen.

One evening they came to a brackish pond. Moralin crouched listlessly by it, thinking about the lake in the middle of the Delagua city, fed by underground streams. It was a place of cool respite except in the evenings when the feverbirds did their hunting along the shoreline. A person who stood under the whooshing of those giant wings was sure to wake up flushed and burning and was often soon dead.

Excitement rustled through the camp as people crushed shells and made a paint to decorate their bodies, using their fingers or tufts of grass to form patterns. That night no one built a fire, and the painting and chanting went on and on. By the time the ugly half-moon went down, everyone had a yellow body. Some had yellow handprints spread over their cheeks to look like feathers. Others had fish fins painted around their eyes.

At dawn fish leaped from the water in spiraling arcs. People spread nets among the floating weeds. Soon yellow birds circled and came in to rest on the water, a flock so huge that Moralin thought a person, stepping on their backs, could run out to the middle of the pond. People waded through yellow feathers that swirled around their ankles and stuck to them. Lan would love the feathers. Moralin caught one, but after a few moments she dropped it and watched it blow away.

She saw that some of the girls were carrying the birds in nets. Pity for them and for herself, poor prisoners all, made her choke. She watched fish being strung over the fire and cooked. If only she could give up her life as easily as a fish seemed to. The familiar words of the death prayer ran through her mind. Oh, Great Ones, I thank you that you gave me life as a Delagua fighter and not as a shadow or an animal. May I stand with courage and look death in the eyes before I ever bring shame to my people.

The next evening they walked down the slope toward the black mouth of a cave. That night was full of whispers and movements and far-off haunting cries. People lit torches from the embers of a fire and walked off into the midnight-dark cave's throat. The lights flickered, wavered, and were swallowed. A long time later people began to trickle back. She saw that they had been gathering salt.

Near dawn she fell asleep sitting and had a dream so clear she opened her eyes and felt tears on her cheek. First she had been falling, falling through a white mist. She could see the wall of the Delagua city, and she reached out; but under her fingers the stones turned smooth, and she could not hold on. What did it mean? Probably that death would soon come for her.

On the next terrible day she walked through gray ashes that drizzled out of the sky from a far-off fire, making the ground slick and hot. Moralin slipped and slid. When she managed to steady herself, the woman she was tied to would lose her balance, and the two of them would fall again.

Finally the woman untied the thong and used a rock to strike the trunk of a tree. She gathered chunks of sap that had welled up along old bruises. Moralin sucked on a little piece, so bitter it made her mouth ache, but it did take away her thirst.

She touched her wrist tenderly. The rope had rubbed

the skin off. Would it become infected? If so, she would die a weak and feeble death with fever tearing at her body. That was no death for a fighter. Could she somehow coax more freedom from the warrior woman? She pointed to the sap and spoke for the first time in many days. "What is its name?"

The woman ignored her.

She tried again, gesturing with her chin as she'd seen the boy and other people do. It worked.

"*Rikka,*" the woman said without expression.

"*Rikka.*" Next, Moralin lifted the waterskin, pantomimed the act of drinking. The word for water made a little explosion in her mouth as she said it. When the warrior woman laughed at her mockingly, she knew her pronunciation was bad, or maybe she had even said an embarrassing word. And her plan failed. When it was time to go, the warrior woman tied Moralin again.

The next day they met up with another knot of people. At first Moralin assumed they were from the original group. Most Arkera looked the same to her.

But later she decided that these must be people whose rainy season camp had been somewhere else. People sang songs back and forth and touched cheeks with great warmth. Sometimes, from their gestures and glances, she knew they were telling stories about her, her actions by the campfire and how she had tried to escape.

By the time dusk came on that night, a thin smell of fermenting fruit hung in the air. The animals sensed it first. The four-legged ones howled, and the yellow birds stirred and squawked in their nets. People began to sniff and hesitate.

"Kachee," someone shouted.

"Kachee." Others took up the cry.

Moralin looked around. Dying from some kind of animal bite or goring was a good death. People shuffled and shouted, beginning to form a circle. The warrior woman drew a bone knife and, without warning, slashed the thong.

The air filled with a strange clicking sound. The ground began to move as if the dirt had come alive.

Small dark animals scurried forward in a wave, paused, advanced. Moralin strained to see. Bodies a little bigger than men's feet. Whip-thin tails. She made out triangular heads with sharp snouts.

People crowded together and pounded the earth with snakesticks and rocks, shouting a *hoo-hoo* chant. A woman rushing toward the group dropped a net, and yellow birds fluttered out, helpless with their feet tied together. Moralin watched as dark shapes pooled around the birds and dragged them away.

This was her chance to die. But when the first kachee leaped at her, she couldn't offer up her throat as she'd planned but automatically flailed at it, crying out as the claws ripped the flesh of her hands.

She lurched back. Bumped into the warrior woman. Using the woman's back as a brace, she groped for anything. Felt something—a spear? a branch?—under her fingers. She swung it with all the force of a fighting stick and felt the thud as she connected. Swung again. And again. To her shame, something inside her seemed determined to stay alive.

Gradually the clicking died away. Moralin swiped the sweat from her eyes and smelled the blood on the back of her hand. It was now too dark to see much of anything, but the kachee seemed to be gone. Only the smell hung everywhere.

The warrior woman rubbed healing oils into Moralin's hands. That night she did not tie Moralin up. The next morning she did not bind their wrists together.

As she walked, Moralin considered just running. The warrior woman's spear would be quick. Or would Old Tamlin want her to die proudly, standing to face her enemies? He had always admired the prisoners who were brave as they were killed in the Delagua city.

She lost count of the times she fell, the times she put her head on a rock at night and pulled a blanket over it, too tired to eat. When conversations washed over her, she noticed that the boy had been right. By listening for familiar words and watching gestures, she could sometimes make out pieces of a story, such as one about when the dry times came early.

The Arkera had apparently been caught on this part of the journey, no chance to get to deep mother. A story-teller coughed and choked, showing the heat and dryness. She acted out dust descending like huge birds, covering the Arkera.

At the end of the story people chanted something. Perhaps, "Do not give us such a year"? Moralin smiled grimly, stone-hard inside. She would be glad of another such year and would pray for it to come. Let her enemies choke with thirst, even if she choked, too.

The next day they traveled in swirling grit. She could barely make out other gray shapes around her. At the top of a slope she looked back and saw they had crossed a finger of yellow-brown sand. Dust hung over it in a haze.

For the rest of the day they climbed in a rough country of canyons and small cliffs. When she raised her eyes, she saw a butte that held back the sky. She trudged for hours, legs aching. Finally the way seemed to be blocked by a wall ahead, but when they reached it, the warrior woman led her into a narrow passageway.

People called out, their voices echoing against the

rocks. The woman in front of her began to move faster, faster, faster . . . to what? Rock loomed on either side, close enough so she could touch the walls with both hands. She found the strength to follow up a long set of rock stairs, natural or man-made. Faster. Faster. When she half-fell out the other end of the chute, she gasped and staggered back. An enormous skulkuk's eyes glared down at her.

Be strong. It was only painted onto a rock. Around it crouched other monsters that Moralin had never seen, not even in tapestries.

The woman guided her onto a narrow path that led around the painted rock. Without warning they were looking down into a wide, flat canyon. Moralin bent over, trying to catch her breath from the climb. This must be the place of her death—in the belly of Arkera deep mother.

CHAPTER EIGHT

As they reached the bottom of the canyon, they splashed through a stream, surely smaller than in the rainy season, but still with good water. Ahead, Moralin saw houses wearing their roofs pulled down low like hats made of grass. The warrior woman led her to one and pushed her inside. The walls were mud with pieces of straw sticking out, and the floor was polished hard clay. One wall was yellow with moss. Outside, the smell of meat over a fire made Moralin dizzy with hunger.

She was alone. Now she could finally grieve. Go ahead. Weep. She waited for the hardness to dissolve. Nothing happened. So she sat with her back against the mossy wall. People were running between houses. Everyone seemed to be trading stories and laughing.

When darkness dropped, a woman appeared at the doorway and beckoned. Outside, Arkera thronged around a crackling fire. After a while the best storytellers were pushed forward. They acted out the adventures with great groans and hisses, somehow capturing even the whir of wings. People laughed and grunted and cheered them on.

Moralin looked around for Salla. There. Was that Salla? Moralin was moving to see more clearly when rough hands grabbed her and pushed her into the crowd. People scrambled out of her way. Near the center someone gave her a hard shove, and she stumbled forward and knelt in the dirt.

Four elders with severe faces stood over her. They all were draped in bright feathers. The man in the green cloak, who had spared her life at the camp, now wore a headdress made of yellow ones. An old woman said something in a hard voice.

Moralin heard a low, hissing noise rise from the crowd. Out of the corner of her eye she caught a flash of firelight on a black knife.

She raised up on her knees as tall as possible. "May I look death bravely in the eyes and not bring shame to my people," she said aloud.

CHAPTER NINE

THE BACK OF HER NECK PRICKLED, BUT THE blow didn't come. Instead the storytellers acted out her story. The attack of the skulkuk started up some argument. She tried frantically to understand. One of the storytellers howled in rage and shook imaginary bars. They had captured it and brought it back here? Surely not. A man gestured to the east. Moralin imagined she heard skulkuk snorts through the chatter.

Finally an elder spoke rapidly, shaking her fist

toward Moralin. Another shouted. Moralin felt the heat of the fire on her scalp and smelled smoke and meat and skins, but it all seemed unreal. One part of the circle bulged, and Figt was pushed into the center. She stood swaying slightly before the elders.

Moralin leaped to her feet, stunned with hatred. She forced herself to not look away from the fevered glare in the eyes of her old enemy. Around the circle people shouted opinions and comments. When the old woman raised her hands high, the murmurs died away. She said something in the voice of whitest doom.

Green Cloak spoke next, but his accent was so terrible Moralin would not have recognized the Delagua words except that he said each one so slowly. "You are brave. You are The People now." He gestured to show what he meant by *The People*. Arkera. He was trying to say, "You are Arkera now."

Her head buzzed. "No," she said softly. "Let me die."

Back in the hut she refused to raise her head from the blanket. Starvation was not a fighter's death, but it was her only choice. How much did it hurt to die that way?

She wondered, again, if they had killed Song-maker. If his people walked the whole flat earth, did they also walk the round sky? It was a comfort to think that perhaps he would appear again to guide her through the strange world of the afterdead.

What about Figt? Whatever the man in the green cloak said had made the girl hang her head with a look even Moralin could tell meant shame and suffering. Perhaps Moralin would have another chance to fight her enemy after death.

For a week Moralin hardly moved. They poured water into her mouth, but they could not make her eat. At first hunger clawed her stomach, but then it went away. She dreamed her life was a huge yellow eye that was slowly closing. Let the dim light leach the red from her blood. Let her teeth darken. Even prayers could do no good in this wretched place so far from the lands the Great Ones watched over.

Outside the hut she heard the musical sound of oil

being poured into clay jars. She could smell fish, probably strung to dry. Inside the hut she heard the whisper and scurry of small animal feet, but she did not see any living things except the women who forced water into her throat, the girls who placed gourds of food near her and rushed away.

One day she slipped into a half-waking state in which she mostly imagined herself back home. White beetles scurried over her hands, and she welcomed them because they spoke to her of death. Once, when she was a little girl and standing with Grandmother in the temple, she'd been frightened by a ghostly figure woven into the tapestry.

Grandmother had turned quickly away. "Such come for us when we die. It's forbidden to look upon them except on tapestries."

"Is it a spirit?"

"No. Only a priestess wearing a dui-dui."

As she got older, she had learned that priests came to the house on the day after death. Sometimes, depending on the time of the moon, the priests carried salts. Other times they carried only jars of spices, beeswax, frankincense, and the golden tree sap that came from a faraway golden city. No one else entered the room. Every time day and darkness came and went twenty-five times, the moon shut its evil eye for three nights, now helpless to steal people's spirits. On the first dark night, the city fell silent. People hid in their houses while priestesses in dui-dui clothing carried the bodies to temple safety. But Moralin would have no one to carry her. Her only hope was that the beetles might whisper of her death to a passing feverbird, and thus the news would finally reach Cora Linga at the temple.

One of the beetles stood near her head. At the tips of its feelers were two orange spots that looked like disapproving eyes. Mother's eyes. "Moralin, why are you sulking?" That's what Mother would say if she were here. "You dishonor the Great Ones when you give up."

"I want to be home," Moralin whispered. "I want to be home."

The orange eyes reproached her. "Do your duty, child."

She turned her head away. How many times had she heard those words? Grandmother said every Delagua was responsible for acting honorably. That was why Mother lived obediently in the house of her husband's family even though her husband did not live there. That was why Old Tamlin had his own house and days full of responsibilities.

Even shadows patiently labored long, hard hours and slept on mats in underground rooms. They appeared happy to trade their work for food and shelter. She could certainly be as dutiful as a shadow.

So she was not supposed to die. What, then, must she do?

"The Great Ones help those who use their own strength," Grandmother often said.

"When you are confused," Old Tamlin said, "begin by listening."

She looked back, but the beetle was gone.

The next morning Moralin listened. Someone was pounding grain. Someone else was sharpening a knife.

Eventually three men began to argue. She heard the word "skulkuk." One of the men kept repeating something. She recognized one of his words from what Song-maker had told her. Young.

If the skulkuk they had taken was young, imagine one full-grown. Why would they risk bringing such a thing into the village?

She shook her head. They were Arkera. Their ways couldn't be understood. After all, why had they carried Salla when they killed the two other girls? Why bring Moralin herself to be a thorn in the flesh?

But girls were not as powerful as that creature. It made no sense to bring something here that had the strength to destroy everything.

Why? she asked again. Why? Why?

That day she stretched her fingers to the food the young girls brought. She listened longer, but by night she still had no answers.

In the darkness she startled awake panting with fear. Once again she saw the skulkuk as she had seen it that day: the wings and clawed feet and webbed red skin.

Then a thought came, slamming her with such force that her weak hand flew to her chest.

The Arkera wanted a skulkuk because only something with wings could lift up and over the walls of a city. They wanted a young one because they believed they could train it to do their bidding. They also wanted highborn Delagua who they arrogantly believed might become Arkera: Salla because she was soft and weak, Moralin because they admired her bravery and thought she had Arkera courage.

Delagua could help them learn the secrets they needed for a successful attack. They were willing to risk everything to have a chance to pull down their old enemies.

Fear pounded on her as if she were a drum. What was she doing, dying in here? She must save her people.

The next morning she woke to feel something tugging at her hair. She moved her head very slowly and instantly heard the sounds of skittering feet. A small gray wood animal quivered near the wall of the house, waiting for the slightest motion from her. After the pulsing of her heart stopped, she was amused to see its twitching watchfulness. She inched her fingers toward a yellow seed left in the gourd where her food had been. In a quick motion she tossed the seed toward the animal. The creature flicked away. But when Moralin closed her eyes again, then opened them quickly, the seed was gone.

After that she saved a bit of whatever food the girls gave her. A little at a time she regained her strength. She coaxed the wood animal closer. As she watched the animal nibble on the bits of food, she thought she must try to be like the wood animal to the Arkera.

Most of the girls dropped the gourd and left, but one hovered near the door to watch her eat. Moralin said *Jaysha*, the Arkera greeting. The child gave her the briefest smile, fish-quick and gone. The next time she came she told Moralin her name was Ooden.

They started by pointing. At first everything made Ooden smile shyly. But Moralin was determined, and she learned rapidly. "Eye." "Head." "Nose." Ooden's hands fluttered, acting out something deep inside that could rise out through the head. "Spirit?" Ooden took a stick and drew a family. *Amma*—that was "mother." *Abbat*. "Father." "Brother." "Sister." Moralin slowly became used to studying the little girl's face and not looking away.

"Can I leave here?" Moralin walked her fingers along the ground.

No. Ooden leaped up to block the doorway, showing that the warriors would come with their sticks.

"Pot." "Stream." "River"—a little to the east. Using gestures, Moralin managed to describe reeds that she had seen by the stream. When Ooden brought the reeds to her, she wove them into a small cage.

The next time the tiny animal sat nearby, nibbling at a bit of fruit, Moralin scooped it up into the cage. From then on she had something to talk to during the long, boring stretches when she was alone. She stroked its smoke-gray softness. She spoke to the animal only in Arkera. At night she drifted to sleep saying Arkera words. One night she dreamed in Arkera and woke smiling.

CHAPTER
TEN

W HEN THEY RAN OUT OF THINGS TO POINT
to in the hut, Ooden brought something new with her
each time. Or with her finger she made pictures in the
dirt. Something to do with *amma* and *abbat*? Moralin
felt a surge of satisfaction the day she figured out a
word that Ooden often said. "Ancestors."

Words of movement and being were harder. Ooden
acted things out. Words built on words. Once Moralin
had learned "beast" and "warrior," Ooden taught her

"fear" and "courage," giggling as she acted out the menacing beast and brave warrior.

Other words were exasperating. "Bad" was easy. But what was this other one? Worse than bad? "Evil?" Many phrases Moralin couldn't translate precisely but gradually thought she understood. "I like it." "I don't like it." One phrase seemed to be used the way the Delagua said, "Mark it well."

Moralin began to put words into sentences. Experimenting. "Girl grows into woman," she said. Ooden clapped her hands with excitement, then offered a small correction. Moralin tried again.

Ooden kissed her on both cheeks. "This girl now has it exactly right."

One day Moralin pointed at the designs painted on the girl's stomach. "What are these?" At first, Ooden just giggled. When Moralin coaxed, Ooden gave some brief explanation. The only words Moralin recognized were "plant" and "work." She sighed and gestured for Ooden to try again.

"Very soon . . ." Ooden rattled on. "Moon." "Fire."

Ooden pulled out her bottom lip between two fingers, tugging at it. "Courage." Was she talking about some kind of ceremony?

Moralin pointed at herself. "Can I"—she gestured to show that she meant "go through," in Delagua, she finished—"this initiation or whatever it is?"

Ooden frowned. "The ancestors don't like that."

"But . . ." Moralin groaned with frustration. Sometimes she thought she was doing so well, and then she remembered everything she didn't know. Finally she simply said, "Give it to me?" The girl's eyes flicked to her face and then away. She stood up and ran out.

Ooden did not come back. Moralin missed her quick smile and hopping ways. Now that she had decided to live, she ached to see sun, to bathe in a stream, anywhere, even without soap. Her skin itched. Her hair felt heavy and dirty. Three other young girls brought food, and she spoke to them, even though they laughed at her mistakes. Their voices reminded her of the Delagua girls who teased her while their mothers and grandmothers were weaving together. "Are you a boy?" they would ask in soft, mean voices as she stood awkward and impatient at the loom. "Ask your mother to check."

On a warm night Moralin lay awake for a long time. She thought she heard the moans of the skulkuk, far off, but perhaps it was someone blowing a shell. The pongas began thrumming again. By now the wood animal was so used to her it hardly moved when she stroked its silk fur and tickled its nose. She took it out of the cage and let it run up her arm, laughing at the feeling of its tiny star-shaped, straw-scratching feet on her skin. Finally she fell asleep thinking of Song-maker's lessons long ago. "I ran. Thee ran. You ran. She ran. He ran. They ran. We ran."

She jerked awake when someone touched her shoulder. It was Ooden. The upper part of her face was painted red. A red line ran from under her nose to her chin.

Ooden held her finger to her lips and beckoned.

Moralin stumbled out of the house. The moon was a red bowl in the sky, huge and soft. The pongas were loud, and fire crackled and leaped.

All the people, even the babies, were painted with red, yellow, and black designs. Moralin followed, and Ooden slipped close to the fire, where she stood silently along with eleven other girls. People began to trill. An old woman stepped forward. She spoke softly to each girl, then bent and scooped something out of a basket. It seemed to pour itself down her arm, rippling like a lake's wavelets. Moralin licked her lips. Manage your fear.

The woman stretched her arm into the air. The snake writhed and wrapped itself around her hand. Its black eye glared. The woman handed the snake to one of the girls. The girl lifted it high as the old woman chanted: "I speak for this child to our brother snake, sister snake. One who . . ." Moralin frowned at the words she didn't know.

"Oh, ancestors, give her courage," the woman chanted.

Moralin hid her smile, remembering Ooden acting out a wild beast, arms high, fingers stiffened into claws.

"May she be . . ." The woman said an unfamiliar word. "Worthy," Moralin finished to herself. It must be. That's what the Delagua would say.

Ooden took the snake. The painted lines across the girls' mouths must mean they should not talk or cry out.

Next, the old woman took something—a sharpened bone?—from the hot coals. She used it to pierce the first girl's lower lip and moved to the next girl, leaving the bone in place. None of the girls flinched or gasped.

At the end the painted lines were wiped away. "These children are worthy," the old woman called out. "Mark it well." She began to paint a red leaf shape on the first girl's stomach. The circle burst into a high, shrill joy cry. The sounds shimmered in the air as she painted.

Soon Ooden was back. The girl's eyes were shiny in the firelight. "I was worthy," Ooden said. "Go forward and be worthy, too. He calls."

Moralin hesitated. What would she have to do to be worthy? The smoke seemed to form itself into the thin head and wide, baleful eye of a snake.

"Go," Ooden whispered. Moralin swallowed and took a step.

"Who speaks for her?" Green Cloak asked.

To Moralin's surprise, the warrior woman came forward. "This is my story." She said something about the kachee. Moralin heard voices crying out, "True, true."

Ooden stepped gingerly forward. "This is my story. She knows many words." The man's eyes seemed to burn Moralin's face, already slippery with sweat. Could she convince him she had changed? He held up a pouch and asked for its name. The whole circle seemed to watch her with one fierce eye. She took a deep breath and said the name, hoping she had pronounced the word close to right. She heard muffled laughter near the back.

The man held up one thing after another. "This girl says thee wishes to become one of The People. True?"

"True." She looked briefly into his eyes.

"We ask the fire to give us a sign." He motioned, and two men took sticks and pulled coals from the fire, a terrible orange-red path dusted with gray. Moralin shrank back. Grandmother had spoken of this barbaric custom, walking on fire. The stories said some survived. Others were badly burned. She could almost smell the stink of her own burning flesh.

Green Cloak folded his arms. The orange glissim of the coals made her sick with terror.

She forced herself to breathe calmly. She looked up at the moon, heard the far-off cries of tree animals, a wailing like a weird wind. How many times had Old Tamlin tried to get her to master her fear of high places and climb the wall? "Name your fear," he would say.

"It's a muddy river, pouring through my heart."

"Go into that river. Turn the mud to solid ground. Climb upon it."

She had never been able to go into the river of fear. Could she do it now? She made all her thoughts and feelings go up, up into the whirling in her head. Slowly she made the waves and trickles stop. The mud hardened. She saw herself, now a small girl, climb out. Sit on top. "Mamita," the little girl on the solid river whispered over and over. "Help me."

The child in her head watched as Moralin walked calmly to the coals. She was silent and fearless as Moralin raised her foot and set it right down on the coals and then walked quickly, steadily across.

Moralin was startled by the joy cry. Now the elder raised his hand. "This girl," he said, "has entered the path to become one of The People. Her name will be Kadu."

He looked to Moralin. She said nothing, even though his words cut a hole in her heart.

"Mark it well," the man cried loudly.

"Mark it well," the people echoed.

When their gazes turned away, Moralin quickly checked the bottoms of both feet. Nothing. Not one small blister.

The next storyteller wrinkled her face and popped

her eyes wide open as she told her tale, making those around the fire shriek with laughter. Moralin followed Ooden out of the circle. At the back she caught a glimpse of Figt. The girl, thin and unhappy, hung back from the rest. Moralin felt a flutter of triumph. No beastie. Good. The skulkuk must have killed it.

Ooden showed her the longhouse where she would now sleep. "Yes," Moralin said, and then: "Wait." She ran to the place where she had stayed, lifted the reed cage and looked at the wood creature. Its nose twitched. Her chest crackled with sadness, a sadness so hot that if she had been a Great One, she would have been able to turn herself to fire and rain down on this village.

She fumbled with the hair that tied the door shut. "I'm not to be a prisoner anymore," she whispered. "You mustn't be either. Go well, small friend." She opened the door and watched the animal flick off into a dark corner. As she turned her face to the longhouse, she wondered how long it would be before she felt any stirring of love and care for another creature again.

In the next weeks Moralin came to know the village well. People labored hard for long days always according to their ordered tasks. She shared the house of the young plant keepers.

Each morning the women who were plant keepers gave instructions. The girls knelt and touched their foreheads to the elders' feet. Then they hurried to their work.

Whenever Moralin had a moment to rest, she looked for Salla but found nothing to show the other girl had reached this place alive. Perhaps it was just as well, Moralin thought sadly. If she was right about the skulkuk, better that the Arkera not have soft Salla to pry information from.

Stay alert, she told herself. Find a plan. Whenever adults weren't around, she tried to ask questions or coax Ooden to show her things. "The ancestors don't like that," Ooden was quick to say.

So she watched the young plant keepers as they ate, worked, did their body painting, adding more leaves and brightening up the old ones. When she dared, she peeked inside the little houses around the edge of the village, filled with yellow seed and with other food— green globes, brown pods, scarlet legumes.

Cloth was made from sheets of bark taken from the red trees. Young boys soaked the sheets and then laid them over a log and beat them with wooden mallets. No wonder the cloth was ugly. The yellow birds from the lake were scratching in the dirt now and giving up their eggs. Tame, Moralin thought scornfully, the way she would never be tamed.

She learned to answer to her new name, but she never used it in her thoughts. Although she could understand far more than she could speak, she forced herself to be bold about trying new words even if she appeared foolish. The day she tried the word for "wife" and said the word "termite," instead, most of the young girls shouted with laughter.

"Stop," Ooden told them gravely.

They ran off, still laughing.

Whenever people taunted her for her mistakes, she

smiled, but only with her mouth. I will soon have hold of your powers and your secrets, she told herself.

By the time another full-eyed moon came and went, no one had yet approached her for any kind of information. She did not think Green Cloak would tap her shoulder and say, "Come tell us everything of the Delagua city so we may better plan our attack." But she had hoped she might uncover some small clue to how she could save her people.

How long did she have? She watched women pounding yellow seeds in hollow cylinders, their sticks moving urgently up and down in tune with their chanting, and thought the sticks were like her own heart. She had to know more. Quickly.

"Does everyone go to the camps when the rains come?" she asked Ooden.

The girl hesitated and then told her that most were needed to grow and gather food, but some stayed back.

What if Green Cloak's plan was to get answers from her and then leave her behind?

Finally she was allowed to go with Ooden and the others to the place above the village where they gathered plants. Now she could study the shape of the land. She looked out over the rough buttes to the faint outline of mountains beyond. Those must be the Brown Turtle Mountains. The red forest was to the left of the range. To the right lay a slash of chasm and the ginger-brown land that was said to dry people's lifeblood and leave them shriveled lumps. From up here the sun turned a faraway haze of brown sand-dust into something golden and beautiful.

Pretending to work, Moralin tried out one plan and then another. Make them trust her enough to take her with them if they attacked the city? At the least they must choose her to be among those who went to the red forest when the rains returned. Starting now she'd be ready for anything. She'd begin by making a small store of supplies.

That evening she crept out to the eastern fields and drew close to the place where the skulkuk was held in a huge cage. Bones littered the ground. The Arkera were feeding it, of course, hoping to gain its trust that way. It didn't seem much bigger. Skulkuks must grow slowly.

It lifted half-grown wings at her and growled in its throat. Its purplish eyes gaped, sharp and malevolent. But she felt only sadness for it. Even an ugly creature belonged somewhere. Probably under its dark scales, it, too, longed to go home.

On her way back she saw Figt, scuttling along the eastern fields, alone except—Moralin was surprised to see—for the beastie at her heels. So it hadn't died. Was the girl spying on her?

Moralin's favorite place became the clifftop above the village, where they dug and gathered roots and plants, soaking in the smells of their savory leaves. Anything that seemed helpful she slipped into a pouch that she carried with her always. Sometimes she sat for a moment with her toes buried in the warm earth, watching Ooden, thinking about Lan. Did her little sister miss her? Did they all assume her dead?

When the girls fell silent, working hard, the only

sound was creaking birdsong. One particular call reminded Moralin of Song-maker's flute.

Quite often the girls laughed and shoved one another playfully. Then she remembered the times, long ago, when the house owned by her grandmother was full of wonderful smells and good food, and the servants spoiled Moralin, letting her run among their vats of dye—even if she spilled them—smiling indulgently when she became demanding. Her mother and grandmother moved on the edges of the rooms, always serene, always beautiful, always a little mysterious. When they took her to visit Old Tamlin's house, he made no secret, even then, that he thought her special.

Later she and her mother had rubbed like sand against each other. Now Moralin could hardly remember what they had argued about, except Mother was so disappointed she hated the weaving work. "Mamita," Moralin murmured often, choosing to use the name from when she was little.

Slowly the plant keepers seemed to accept her presence with them. She let them comb her hair with the red oil that kept it from flying in her face. They showed her green seeds she could eat when she needed to work long hours without falling down from tiredness and where to dig for insects that were made into paste for stomach illness. She learned the uses of many herbs.

Each day brought hard work, more than she had ever done at home, where shadows did the back-bending chores. But work made her arms and legs stronger and kept her thoughts from wandering to fearful places.

One dry afternoon the herb gathering led them high above the village. She and Ooden wandered far from the others, following a bird that Ooden said would lead them to a food of shining sweetness. Moralin was pushing branches aside when she heard Ooden hiss sharply. She stopped.

Ooden stood as if her feet had turned into roots.

Moralin squinted. She took a cautious step forward.

"No," Ooden whispered. "Do not even turn thy head toward that place."

Moralin had never seen the other girl frightened like this. "What is it?"

Ooden was wheezing slightly. The air was hazy, but Moralin thought she could make out a chasm. She took another step. "Stop," Ooden said, but she made no move to stop Moralin.

"What? An animal?"

Ooden opened her mouth but seemed unable to speak.

"A poison plant?" Whatever this terrible danger was, she needed to know.

A breeze stirred the dust. Was that some kind of swaying rope bridge that covered the chasm? Maybe enemies of the Arkera lived on the other side of that log. So close to the village? Impossible. But then what?

The breeze carried a soft keening sound toward them.

Moralin paused, not wanting to turn her back on danger. "Run!" Ooden shouted. They crashed through the brush. A whiff of something odd lifted the hair on the back of Moralin's neck. She risked a quick glance behind her, but nothing that she could see or hear was chasing them.

Ooden slowed, reaching for Moralin's hand.

"What is it?"

"The place of the dead." Whatever Moralin asked, she would say nothing more except "Tell no one where we were."

Late that night, when everyone seemed to be asleep, Moralin stared into the darkness, feeling the prickles of fear all over again. Ooden, on the mat beside her, moaned and moved in her sleep.

Moralin touched the other girl's arm.

Ooden sat up, wiping at her eyes. Moralin handed her a waterskin and then whispered, "Why not tell the other girls about today?"

Ooden spoke in a shocked, low voice. "The ancestors don't like it." She lay down again with a whimper, and soon Moralin heard from her breathing that she was asleep.

CHAPTER

ELEVEN

THE NEXT MORNING OODEN LOOKED PALE
and restless. "This morning we dry herbs," she told
Moralin. She walked off, not her usual friendly self.
As they worked, Ooden didn't join in the other girls'
chatter. After a while, intense and serious, she began
to instruct Moralin. By watching Ooden's face and
gestures, listening for words she knew . . . and
guessing . . . Moralin decided the girl was telling her
about how workers were assigned to each village, but
the system seemed to depend on complicated family

lines and patterns that Moralin couldn't figure out.

"Who takes the bodies to the place of the dead?"

Ooden glanced at her unhappily and changed the subject. "Know that one who came with thee to The People?"

The other girls were chittering together, paying no attention. "I know," Moralin said.

"She is in another village. Married."

"So young?" Moralin swallowed, trying not to show her shock. "Is that . . ." What was the word for "custom"? Salla? Truly becoming Arkera? How could she?

"And the warrior girl who was watching thee. Remember her?"

"No." The word burst out too quickly, but Ooden didn't seem to notice.

"She was to become a warrior because her mother and father died. Orphans make the best fighters." Ooden's voice was matter-of-fact. "If they fight well, a new family line is set up for them. Now she is a solitary."

"And what work can a solitary do?"

"No work. Those who do not work are given no food. Soon—" Ooden stopped. "Come. Don't talk of such things." She jumped up. "This is the afternoon for gathering mantur berries."

The thought of mantur berries seemed to make everyone happy. Even Ooden brightened as they ran for their baskets, not beautiful, graceful Delagua baskets, just ugly ones of woven reeds. As they started up the path from the village, an old woman blocked their way. Each girl greeted the woman respectfully, but when the old woman shook her finger at Moralin and began to correct her pronunciation, only Ooden waited while the others ran on.

"Listen," the woman continued. "This is my story." She'd had a dream the night before, a terrible dream of a monster coming out of the sky. "Beware," she said. "Tell the other girls. Thee goes to the other girls? Tell them to beware." Then she recited the dream again, from beginning to end.

Moralin did not know how to move without being disrespectful. Finally, though, Ooden interrupted the woman to ask, "Should we not go then? Warn the others?"

The old woman walked away, muttering. But when they reached the fork in the path that led to the cliff tops, they could see no one. Ooden frowned. "I am wondering why she told us and not the elders."

"True," Moralin said. "The other girls are far beyond us now."

Ooden smiled for the first time that day. "Here is something my mother showed me."

They ran back to the village and pushed their way through some brush into a small side canyon. Ooden ducked behind a huge rock. A moment later Moralin saw that Ooden was climbing, balancing between the trunk of a slender tree and the rock.

When she was high up the tree, she reached for the cliff wall. "It's one of the old ways The People used," she called. "The People know everything about climbing."

Moralin made herself step toward the rock. "What?" she whispered to herself, as Old Tamlin would. "Have you lost your courage?" She scrambled after Ooden, blocking out the fear. Up the tree. Yes, she could feel the handhold on the cliff wall.

Think of nothing but the wall. The holes were easy, perfectly spaced, and well dug. She climbed up three steps. Then the trembling began. "I can't do it," she called.

Ooden was halfway up the cliff, climbing quickly and surely. "Kadu, come."

"I can't." Moralin tried to ease herself back down. When she finally was on the ground, she sat, holding on to her shaking knees, pulling her imagination back from where it *would* make her go, dangling high above the ground and screaming.

CHAPTER

TWELVE

Ooden made a sad-eye face. "The others will have the mantur berries all picked."

"We should . . ." Moralin wiggled her fingers away from her mouth, trying to remember the words. "The old woman?"

Ooden clicked her tongue impatiently and indicated the cliffs above the village, where warriors kept constant watch. If the villagers ever heard the moaning note blown on a shell, everyone would know danger was upon them.

Just before they reached the mats where herbs were drying, one of the adult plant keepers called Ooden over to help carry some gourds. As soon as the girl was out of sight, Moralin bent, searching for the things she most wanted for her pouch.

When she saw Ooden coming, she hastily squatted and pretended to be busy. Ooden dropped down and rested her head against Moralin's arm, rubbing with her finger at a drop of sweat. "Hot today," Moralin said. "May the rains come soon."

"My mother says on such a day the earth spirits fought with the air spirits. The People had to hide in their houses until the ancestors sent a thunderstorm to split the earth open. The spirits tumbled in." Ooden tumbled backward, showing Moralin what she meant.

When Moralin laughed, Ooden shook her finger. "No, don't upset the ancestors. The split is still there, between the red forest and the sand waste."

"The People do what in the little rains?" Moralin asked.

Ooden made her hands into claws, showing the way

the warriors would dance, tuning their spirits to the animal spirits that they would hunt for the village's meat. "That one"—Ooden pointed with her chin at a warrior squatting nearby—"he wears snake spots on his back." Her eyes were wide and amazed. "To learn snake secrets."

Moralin waggled her hand, palm down, the Arkera gesture for understanding. Yellow paint. Yellow birds.

"Long ago only men danced and hunted." Ooden tenderly sifted a handful of herbs. "Then, my mother says, the men all disappeared. Women had to learn to dance with big, manlike steps. Now they can be given a warrior path."

They worked silently for a few moments. "Hungry and thirsty will soon seize us?" Moralin asked.

Ooden jumped up. "We have rikka sap. Wait. I'll show you."

Fingering the sticky chunk Ooden held out, Moralin remembered the day she'd tasted it. Was she even the same person? When Ooden wasn't looking, she put the sap into her pouch. Pay attention. Be ready for the unexpected.

The next day a hot, swirling wind scorched the village, carrying stinging dust in its teeth. Ooden showed Moralin how to cover her nose and mouth with a cloth that had been soaked in tree juice. After the plant keepers had spread extra hides over the drying herbs and weighted everything well, the girls sat in the longhouse playing a game.

Moralin was tossing a rock into the air and trying to scoop up a second before the first one hit the ground when Ooden looked at her and said, "This Kadu does not look like us."

Surprised, Moralin dropped both rocks.

"Wait." Ooden grabbed a facecloth and ran outside. She returned with pods that the girls squeezed between their hands until a thin, clear liquid ran into a gourd. They brightened their own designs. Then Ooden turned to the girl named Nazeti. "Cover her eyes," Ooden told her, reaching to pull back Moralin's hair.

Moralin tried not to laugh as small brushes tickled her face. She watched the leaf designs appear on her forearms and hands. The girls stood around her, admiring their work. Curious fingers reached out to tug a hair on her arm. Moralin pretended to growl, and Nazeti leaped back, shrieking. For a moment there was silence.

Then somebody pushed somebody else, and Moralin found herself in the middle of a warm, wiggling pile. They giggled and wrestled until they were tired. That night, just before she fell asleep, Moralin felt a small hand slip into hers.

The next morning she stepped to the door of the longhouse, smiling. Something was different. No, it wasn't. The village was moving in its morning rhythms, small fires smoldering, mothers murmuring to their babies. In the light she studied her bright arms and hands.

Then a long, low note moaned. Moralin stared up at the cliffs. A child shrieked.

Another note answered the first. "Seek water." Shouts sang out. "The river." Instantly the village began to pound with running feet.

She whirled and saw that the young girls were already right behind her. Another long, low note moaned. Moralin looked for a moment into Ooden's wide, scared eyes. "Go. I will come."

Inside, she knelt and rolled the blanket, forcing her fingers to be calm. She grabbed the soaked cloth and wrapped it around her head, fumbled for her pouch and a waterskin, and then rushed back to the door.

By now people were tripping over one another in air thick with panic. Babies were wailing. An animal barked wildly, and another began to howl. *Bold enough?* Someone that looked a little like Figt ran by, and Moralin made up her mind. Whoever would attack the Arkera was a friend of hers. She dashed in the opposite direction.

As she ran, a whistling roar drowned the other noises, louder and louder, then so loud she covered her ears and ducked into a hut, yelping in fear. She peeked out. An immense skulkuk, even bigger than the one painted on the canyon wall, was sweeping toward the village with fire streaming from its mouth.

For a moment everything was trembling and noise. The roar died. Moralin saw that the roofs of several houses near her were on fire.

She ran again, coughing, dodging fires that sprouted everywhere. When she was almost to the side canyon, the skulkuk passed over the village from the west. She heard its scream and an answering scream from the eastern fields.

Run. Her feet were heavy and hot. Her eyes streamed salt. Her chest felt like fire itself, but she didn't slow down. Ahead, the slender tree was smoking. Heat ripped her hands as she climbed.

This time she didn't pause until she reached rock. For one awful moment she clung to the swaying tree. A faint memory of Old Tamlin's voice brought her back to herself.

Falling from the cliff would be better than being burned up in the skulkuk's fire or wasting away in an Arkera village. If she was going to die, she could die a Delagua death.

Up she went, groping for unseen handholds, barely

aware of the supplies that flapped around her waist. At the top she grabbed handfuls of grass and hauled herself over.

She rolled away from the edge and looked back. A sick feeling twisted her stomach. "Old Tamlin," she gasped. "I did it."

Beneath her the village was a mass of fire. A pleasant smell of burning herbs and roasting meat wafted upward as if this were some feast day. How would they rebuild the village, now with the dry times upon them? Had Ooden and Nazeti and the other girls made it to the river?

She staggered to her feet, pulling the cloth from her head, panting. Arkera problems weren't hers anymore. She would have a hard enough time just finding food to keep herself alive.

As she groped in her pouch for the helicht plant to rub on her blistered hands, far away she saw the skulkuk climbing in the eastern sky, only a black blotch from here. Behind it trailed a smaller blotch. So . . . the mother skulkuk had come for its young one after all.

She gave a shout. Then fear slammed her. Just because one prisoner escaped did not mean the other would. After the fires were out . . . the Arkera were excellent trackers.

She felt like a plant suddenly split. How could the unexpected have come this fast? She'd have to find a plan. For now just get as far as possible from the village.

Her feet seemed to know where to go. Of course. Before long she could see the gorge. She didn't pause until she reached the bridge, where she slid one foot onto the woven ropes that seemed sickeningly fragile, dancing high above the ground.

Her fingers found the hand rope. She closed her eyes and carefully moved the other foot forward. Winds swept from below, and under her the bridge swayed perilously with each step. Pay attention. Manage your fear. She crept forward, ignoring the choked sound of her breathing.

Out over the deep gorge she imagined that she could feel the air grow thin. Her head was floating. Only the bridge held her to the earth.

Something whispered that she should let go, but her hands kept edging along. She was a Delagua spider, high in the air, clinging to her web. Finally she felt the air grow thick again, and she swallowed it in noisy gulps.

When her foot touched earth, she opened her eyes, grabbed the branch of a nearby bush, and pulled her heavy body off the bridge. She stumbled forward.

Into Arkera death.

CHAPTER THIRTEEN

Death was everywhere. She smelled it. It choked the air and made her faint.

In the trees before her, something clinked softly in the wind. She didn't dare guess what it was.

She began to walk quickly, singing a Delagua war song Old Tamlin had taught her. If the only way home was through Arkera death, so be it.

As she reached the first tree, the air around her crackled with a high, faint sound. She sternly told her foot to lift, advance. Speaking loudly in Delagua, she said, "I'm not one of your people. Your taboos and punishments cannot touch me." The sound didn't lessen.

The gaping eye of a skull grinned down at her. A body had been placed in a reed cage that swung from the branches. One of the angry ancestors? Her throat tightened with disgust and fear, but she forced herself to sing louder, watching the ground so she would not look up at the skeletons.

Everyone knew spirits hovered until bodies were wrapped in cloth. A death-white feeling drenched this place.

The hair bristled on her arms, but nothing reached out to grab her. Nothing touched her except the sweat that trickled down the back of her neck and made her want to whirl around and look behind. She filled her mind with her grandfather's face, wrinkled like old fruit, his hawk-fierce eyes that could turn soft and lively with laughter when he looked at her. "Manage your fear," his voice whispered to her.

Her steps created a drumbeat, and she listened to the

sound until it became a kind of rhythm river that pushed her forward. Only once she hesitated—for a large, brown snake that rustled through the grass just ahead of her. She squatted, wary, until it hissed and slithered away. After a while she glanced up and saw one tree without a skeleton. A long time later—or perhaps it wasn't a long time at all—she realized she could look up and not see any bones. But a few trees later a skull grinned. As if Arkera death were reaching after her.

Finally she was sure she had left the place of the ancestors behind. Now she must get quickly off this high ground. "Cora Linga," she said out loud. "How long must I walk before you can hear me and help me again?" No sleeping tonight. Move on.

As blessed darkness wrapped around her, she kept walking. *The moon. The moon.* Forget the moon. She had walked to deep mother under its open eye yet lived. Strange shapes loomed, moving and shifting and making her wince. Keep going. Keep going down.

Even when a bank of clouds blew up and began to extinguish the stars, one by one, she kept lurching forward. Suddenly her left foot came down into emptiness. She relaxed into the fall, as Old Tamlin had taught her. Still, the jolt of the ground knocked her breath away. She began to roll. With the taste of panic hot in her mouth, she grabbed for anything to slow herself, but she tumbled and slid until she thudded against something. Her side burned from ankle to shoulder, where rocks had scraped her.

Close by, she could make out tree roots that swelled out of the ground. After pushing in among them, she struggled to untie the blanket.

A bird screech woke her up in the early morning. She wanted to curl tightly into the roots and whimper. Instead she rubbed her hand gingerly along her thigh, glad for the pain that helped her know she was alive.

Slowly she rolled her blanket and stared at the designs on her arms, thinking again about Ooden. Nazeti. Then she looked around and said a prayer of thanks that she had not tumbled off a cliff in the dark. Searching, she discovered yellow berries. They made her mouth dry but took away the hunger.

Be strong. As she found her stride, the sun came out, and she felt a bubbling of joy. Who would have believed anyone could get free from Arkera deep mother? She laughed out loud, then clapped her hand over her mouth.

If only she had a guide. When did Song-maker's work begin? Had he walked to Arkera deep mother or joined the Arkera somewhere in the red forest? What if he had managed to stay alive? Would he work for the Arkera again? She wondered what he would think when she heard of her escape.

Soon thick brush began to crowd her, and she had to fight for each step. Where the bushes ended, a field of stubby trees hunched like angry little men. She whirled. No one.

Cautiously she skirted the trees. They seemed human. Were they evil spirits in disguise? She didn't dare take her gaze from them. In her fear, she missed the dropoff until she had begun to slide again. She grabbed for wiry branches that stuck out from between rocks like scrawny arms. Pain seared her palms. But better hurt hands than a smashed body. Gasping, she eased herself down, using the branches as if they were pieces of rope to cling to.

Then the branches ran out. She blinked away sweat, trying to see what was below. Finally she let go, slid, and landed with a thump.

It was a while before she could ease onto her back. After she had treated her torn palms and scratches with more helicht oil, she sat up and looked around. Smooth rocks stretched in front of her as far as she could see. This must be the bed of some ancient dried-up lake.

She longed to let out a howling wail. The cliff was too steep for her to climb back the way she had come. But going out onto the lake of rocks, with no tree or other cover in sight, would expose her to any enemy or beast.

Shhh-shhh-shhh. Just try it. Maybe it wasn't so bad. When she took her first step onto the rocks, they clacked under her feet with a loud, grating noise. She jumped off. Back at the cliff, she grabbed a handful of grass and tried to hoist herself up; but the roots pulled loose, and she fell backward.

While the sun crawled high into the sky, she stomped up and down the shore, waving her arms in frustration, looking wildly for some other way.

Eventually she rubbed her head, scowling at the rocks. No choice. But every footstep made her grimace. When she slipped, the rocks crackled even more loudly.

She stopped, squatted low against the rocks, and thought about what would come next. Impossible to get far in this dry time, because moving among trees without leaves, she would be nearly as vulnerable and visible as she was here on this lake of stones. What about the cave where the Arkera had gotten salt? Could it shelter her until rainy season? Food. What was salt without food?

Sweating, she stood and went clumsily on. After a long time she thought she could make out gray shapes against the horizon. Rocks? Trees? She balanced on one foot and prodded her sandal to dislodge a pebble.

Click. Someone or something was walking on the rocks behind her.

She stood stone-still. The clicking stopped.

Cautiously, she looked around. Nothing. Well, it couldn't sneak up on her. If she could be heard, she could also hear. She wobbled hastily on. When she could clearly see gray ghost trees ahead, she dropped all caution.

Rushing now. Forward on the tottering rocks. She leaped off the last one and began to run. Trees, even leafless, would give her some cover. Over her panting, she thought she could hear the clicking of stones.

All afternoon she traveled fast. Moving down, always going down. She didn't stop to eat, gulping a swallow or two of water as she walked. The silence was broken only by the rustling of creeping things and other sounds of small animals, but she felt sure something was still following.

Down.

Night began to come on. As the sun dropped, a

breeze blew up. At least the half-moon was draped with a soft gray cloth of clouds.

Something sushed behind her. She whirled. Only leaves, lifted by a sudden gust.

The ground became uneven, pocked with holes. After she had fallen for the third time, she gave a despairing cry.

No banks. No exposed roots. These sleek trees were too thin to climb. Anyway, she didn't want to touch them. She looked up. The breeze kept trying to tug the clouds away. *The moon. The moon.* Forget the moon. It was the least of her worries. She curled in a small depression in the ground, wishing for a weapon.

Something big was still moving through the woods. She was sure of it.

Or was it only the wind in the noisy leaves?

FOURTEEN

SHHH-SHHH-SHH. SHE MADE HERSELF TURTLE-small under her blanket. Her legs quivered as if they belonged to some frightened animal and not to her. Calm. Manage your fear.

But she was absolutely sure she did hear soft footsteps. She threw back the blanket and jumped up. Better to face it standing up.

She stared into the darkness, waiting. Her arms tingled. Nothing. Nothing but the creaking of night insects. Then the thing was rushing out from the ghostly trees. It had hands, hands that reached for her.

She and the thing struggled, bending, turning, gripping, and grabbing at each other until Moralin got the hold she had used on the woman by the fire and flipped her enemy onto the ground. The cloud moved from the face of the moon as the thing groaned.

It was a girl whose eyes glittered and whose painted face she knew. Figt reached up and yanked Moralin's wrist. "This Delagua girl must come back with me."

Fire-fierce rage roared in Moralin's ears, but the other girl gave a hard tug, and she lost her footing. First she was on her knees, then spitting out dirt, then struggling to get free from the beast of a girl who was biting and scratching and trying to pin her to the ground.

All the hard work in the Arkera village had made Moralin stronger, but Figt surely had a knife. She tried not to imagine the stab, the pain sliding into her. Then Figt grabbed a handful of hair, and Moralin screeched and scratched.

They fell apart, panting. Moralin staggered upright,

glaring down. Figt's face twisted, and Moralin whirled to look behind her. But only the beastie appeared, loping through the leaves.

Moralin clamped her hands to her hips so Figt couldn't see them shaking. "You can't make me go back." She used the insulting lower form. Was it true? Figt could kill her with the knife. But could even a warrior girl drag a dead body over the lake of stones and up a cliff?

Perhaps Figt was thinking the same thing. She said nothing, only crawled to a nearby tree. The beastie trotted over and curled on her feet. Figt seemed to fall asleep instantly, sitting up. Moralin took a step toward her, reaching out gingerly. Could she find the knife? She pulled back. Figt would no doubt wake at the slightest touch. The girl's closed fists rested on her knees, fingers curled as though she were begging.

The next morning Moralin ate yellow berries she had stored in her pouch, considering what to do next. Figt crouched nearby and watched. The beastie seemed to be laughing, its panting tongue hanging from its mouth.

Figt was the first to break the silence. "Saw thee when the village was in flames. Saw what was in thy heart." She glanced at Moralin with scorn. "Thy tracks were easy to follow."

"Thee walked on the . . . ?" Moralin made the shape of a bridge with her hands.

"I have no fear of it," Figt said stiffly.

Moralin looked at her curiously. Why not? And what now? If she tried to leave this place, Figt's knife could be out blink-quick. Even if she could somehow outwit the other girl, where could she go to survive the rest of the dry times? She closed her eyes, coaxing back memories of what she had seen on the journey to deep mother.

The red forest was an impossible barrier between her and the Delagua city. Streams would be dry now, even if leaves hadn't crumbled from the trees.

She crouched and spread out the things from her pouch. A little food. Herbs. A beautiful but useless bead. She had run impulsively, grabbing sweet luck.

Now, whichever way she looked, death stared back at her.

Don't despair. If she managed to get away from Figt and find a way to survive until the Arkera were on the move again in rainy season, she could silently follow one of the small groups through the forest and get back to the camp. Find her way from there to the city.

Figt seemed lost in thoughts of her own, using a stick to make markings in the dirt.

Moralin paced. Eventually she was crazed with impatience. She took one cautious step and then another in the direction she had been going. Three more. Her shoulder blades prickled. But Figt just stood up and fell in behind her, moving when she moved, stopping when she stopped.

Today the slope was more gentle. Birds whistled. Here in the open she wasn't likely to be startled by a snake with its wrinkled gait. In other circumstances she would like this feeling of walking freely under the sun.

Soon they reached a rough place of thorny bushes. A

few trees with gray bark spotted the landscape. Moralin paused, studying a rope-twisted trail in the dirt. "Garrag," Figt said.

The word sounded ugly.

Pretending that she knew what she was doing, Moralin dropped to her knees and studied the pattern. The beastie trotted over and licked her cheek. She shoved him. What should she be looking for?

The beastie gave a yelp and hunched miserably, scratching his ear with one left leg. As Figt bent over to examine him, the wind brought a faint sound of a growl.

Figt froze with her hand still on the beastie's ear.

"Garrag?" Moralin leaped to her feet.

Figt gave her head the shake that to the Arkera meant "yes" and to the Delagua meant "no."

No time to ask what to do or why. Figt started to run. Moralin and the beastie dashed after her. Sounds—growling, clicking—erupted around them. Her nostrils filled with the choking smell of fermenting fruit.

A few steps ahead Moralin saw Figt scoop up the

beastie and lift it into a crevice in the side of the butte. She scrambled after and managed to get her own shoulders into the opening by the time sharp claws stabbed her leg. She kicked wildly. The beastie began to bark with a coughing, frantic sound. Moralin dug her straining fingers into the dirt.

She wiggled all the way into the trench and curled into a sitting position, looking over her shoulder. The ground below was a mass of squirming bodies, scrambling over one another. She recognized the sharp snouts and whip-thin tails of the kachee. The clicking pounded on her ears.

Then, with a jolt, the clicking stopped. Silence, followed by a loud, throaty growl. Figt squeezed beside her in the narrow trench, straining to see what was happening.

The grass began to ripple. The gray-green animal that waddled into view on powerful, stubby legs was about as long as two men. It had a great snout with bone-jagged teeth visible all up and down it, even though the thing's mouth was closed.

The wave of kachee began to flow the other way. The garrag waded into the squirming mass and whuffled several into its mouth. Moralin shivered at the *crunch, crunch* of kachee bones. Could the garrag climb? Maybe pain would turn everything blank before the teeth got to her neck.

Figt shoved past.

Moralin scooted back. She could feel blood oozing from her aching leg. Here the trench widened, and dead branches formed a roof. Had this place been made by people? In a moment she heard the soft puff of the other girl's blowpipe and then the garrag's growl of pain.

In the gray light she eased the healing spike from her pouch, peeled the plant's skin back with her teeth, and rubbed her leg, feeling the blood and oils under her fingertips. She couldn't stop shaking. Slowly she loosened her blanket and looked around. Bones gleamed at the back of the trench. Human?

Hunched under the cloth, she let her mind go smooth. She did not think about the garrag, the hopelessness of her situation, or what she was going to try next. Figt took out a small gourd, cupped her hands around it, and blew a soft, mournful note.

When the beastie leaned against Moralin, smelling of dirt and musty leaves, she didn't resist but sat, listening to the sound of its breathing and the sighing of Figt's music.

CHAPTER
FIFTEEN

MORALIN CURLED IN THE CAVE, HALF AWAKE, thinking about the garrag, the hopelessness of her situation, and what she was going to try next. She opened her eyes and squirmed to the mouth of the trench and saw Figt standing on a broad tree branch, gazing into the distance. She was eating something brown, dropping pieces of it to the beastie. "I see the spirit of this dead did not steal thy breath in the night," she said.

Moralin eased out and dropped to the ground. Took a few stiff steps. Her leg was still sore, but the healing oils had done their work. She stooped and picked up a handful of dirt to clean the blood from her fingers.

"Because of the music," Figt added.

Moralin made a noise of disbelief.

Figt climbed down. She didn't offer Moralin whatever she was eating. "All dead spirits want to be dangerous." Her voice was matter-of-fact. "But this music keeps such in their place."

Moralin picked up a piece the beastie had missed. She sniffed at it and took a bite. It was sweet and waxy. Something crunched in her mouth. She tried not to think about what it might be. "Stupid talk," she said.

"Think I'm talking stupid talk? Thee is the stupid one." Figt glared at Moralin with warrior eyes.

Moralin looked around. Had the food come from here? She didn't see any more. Figt must have brought it with her.

The other girl began to talk rapidly. Moralin listened intently, trying to piece together the words and gestures.

Figt had decided not to return to the village. The life of a solitary was . . . she used a word Moralin didn't know, but noting Figt's expression, Moralin almost felt the beginning of pity. Figt continued, talking in such a low, angry voice that Moralin had to strain to catch familiar words. Now Figt had a new plan, and maybe even a stupid one like this girl could be of some use.

"Come." Figt's tone was imperious, but Moralin just shrugged. If anything, they'd been equally stupid.

Once they both were on the low, broad branch she could see that far below them at the foot of the butte the land stretched to the north as if it were a huge piece of quilted cloth. Bare trees of the red forest. Smooth and endless yellow of the sands. The Brown Turtle mountain range and gash of canyon that separated them.

"We go that way." Figt pointed with her chin.

Moralin squinted. "The sand waste? Where no living beings dare go?"

"It is the only way."

The beastie whined and scratched at the foot of the tree. Moralin eased down from the low branch until she was on the ground beside him. Ooden had said, "No work, no food." A solitary might manage to find or steal provisions through one dry season . . . but year after year? It seemed unthinkable, but the Arkera were certainly capable of starving one of their own.

No, it wasn't astonishing if Figt, now that she had shaken free of the village, would decide not to return. But the yellow sands?

Figt dropped, light as a wildcat, and adjusted her waterskin around her waist. "It is the only way, Kadu." Moralin thought she saw fear mixed in with the fierceness on the other girl's face.

"My name is not Kadu. My name is Moralin."

Figt gave her a look she couldn't read. Was it disgust? Was it sadness? "Does this Kadu have a plan?" She grabbed Moralin's wrist.

"Stop!" Moralin pulled away. "Tell me what you . . . tell me what thee wants."

Figt looked off in the distance for a long moment.

162

"When I was young," she said in a strange, halting voice, "my family traveled often in the sands. My mother, my older sister, my little brother, my father."

Moralin turned her head from the pain in Figt's face.

"In those days my people and"—Figt spit—"the dwellers of the sand waste kept clear of each other. We gathered food."

The beastie whined and rubbed against Figt as if it could smell the fierce sadness that seemed to rise from her skin. Figt cleared her throat. "This is my story."

Moralin leaned forward, trying to catch enough words to understand.

One day Figt had begged to stay in the village with her friends. That afternoon The People were attacked in the sand waste. Figt coughed. "My father, my mother . . . the others carried their bodies back to the village."

"Dead?"

"Understand this," Figt said. "When I crossed the bridge, I was not afraid. I knew their spirits would keep me safe."

Dead. Moralin swallowed, remembering whimpers and speared bodies. "Thy brother? Sister?"

"They did not come back."

"How good that thee was not with thy family." It was all she could think to say.

Figt glared at her. "I *should* have been with them." She paused, her face suddenly blank of any expression. "When I wandered alone in the fields, I made a vow to find those who killed them."

So had she now concluded that since she was going to die anyway, she would do it seeking revenge?

"This decision's time has come." Figt chin-pointed at Moralin's pouch. "The plant keepers taught thee things that can help me in the sands. And I can be of use to thee."

Moralin considered. If they survived the sand long enough to find Figt's enemies, Figt could seek a good death by killing some of those who had taken her family.

She herself would most likely also die. But if she managed to survive? She would be among the enemies of the Arkera. Perhaps they would also be allies of the Delagua who could help her find her way home. Her leg was hurting so much it was hard to think, but she looked around for her things.

The ginger-brown and yellow ground that had seemed smooth from high on the cliffs was actually lumpy and rough. Spiny bushes and patches of grass dotted the tan hills. As Moralin climbed down a ragged gash in the land and up the other side, a small whirlwind of sand blew up. When it twirled off, she coughed, spitting out grit. The sky above them was almost white.

Figt gave a wide wave. "The Arkera say that many travelers stand and look upon this place. Those who enter soon have only the hollow eyes of death."

The hollow eyes of death. Moralin hesitated. Maybe she could still find another way.

Figt caught her arm.

Moralin shook herself free. She squatted and picked up a handful of sand. Slowly she let it trickle through her fingers. Might as well die trying to get home.

CHAPTER SIXTEEN

AFTER HOURS OF FOLLOWING FIGT, MORALIN felt as if she had swallowed mouthfuls of sand. By a small gray bush, Figt knelt and began to dig. The beastie joined in, spraying dirt and sand in an arc. Water began to seep into the hole. It was dirty, but Moralin knelt and slurped from both hands. The bright designs were fading. Figt held water in her own hand for the beastie to drink.

They walked on. After a long, dusty time Moralin

knelt and tried digging as Figt had. The beastie helped, just as it had before. But though Moralin stubbornly dug and dug, no water appeared.

Finally, she pulled the rikka sap out and gave each of them a nibble. She held hers in her mouth for a long time, letting the drops leak into her throat. Her feet were swollen rocks. Up and down. Up over a sand dune and down the other side to green and brown patches licked by fat tongues of sand. "Mamita," Moralin whispered through salt-dry lips. She couldn't remember exactly what anyone back home looked like anymore.

Thirst traveled with them always, sometimes a few steps in the distance, sometimes choking their throats. At first Moralin spent her time trying to make plans. In the end she could think of nothing except thirst. Every time she decided she must sink down in the sand and sing her death song, Figt seemed to find a place to dig, some strange plant, a bit of water trapped in the rocks.

With her warrior training, Figt knew little of herbs.

Moralin was the one, using the things from her pouch, who cared for the welts that appeared on their skin from stinging insects, who handed out the hard green berries that gave them strength to walk for hours in the early morning and again as soon as the sun slipped down the sky. "*Nazet,*" Figt told her, holding one up.

"The name of these berries? Like Nazeti, the plant keeper?"

"It's a common name. For a boy, too. It was—" She coughed, a dry, choked sound. "It was the name of my brother."

Moralin nodded. After that, sadness stirred in her every time she took out the berries. Even the beastie learned to chew them.

When they rested in whatever shade they could find, they sat as still as stones, trying not to sweat out precious moisture. During the day they could usually find their bearings from the line of purple mountains. At night Figt used the Arkera constellations: the black-beaked bird and coiled snake, the hunter with his spear, the skulkuk and child.

Moralin no longer felt afraid of the flecked sky. She wished she had listened when Old Tamlin talked about stars. Soldiers had once used them when they needed to capture prisoners for the great ceremonies. Priests still consulted them in temple duties. If she had known she would one day walk openly under the stars, that they could even determine her own life and death, she would have made better use of the moon-dark times when Delagua dared to go outside. She would have learned more than the feverbird with its giant wings spread wide.

Sometimes they traveled in silence, but often it was necessary to talk to stay awake, to keep going. "Tell me about thy city," Figt said one night.

Moralin searched for words to make Figt understand. How huge it was. The strong houses, some covered with flowers, and stone streets with the channels of water running beside. The lake. The temple, which was the center of Delagua life. The fighting yard, where she had been happy.

How to explain Delagua traditions? Not secrets, of

course. Just things anyone could see. That women wore velees when they went outside so their faces would be protected from the eyes of others. That the grinding of flour and the other back-bending work was done by the shadows, wearing masks.

"These masks." Figt interrupted. "Like The People's black-beak masks?"

"No, white. Made of cloth." Soaked in resin, but there was no way to explain that. She showed the way the masks were molded to a shadow's face and allowed to harden. Holes carved for eyes, nostrils, mouths. "The masks do not come off."

Figt stiffened, and Moralin thought the other girl would speak, but she said nothing, so Moralin went on, using words and gestures.

The shadows rarely left their assigned buildings. Never after dark. But then everyone stayed inside most nights, especially those that were eerie silver with moonlight. She paused. No sense trying to explain priests, who studied the stars, or priestesses, who did the work of the dead.

The rest of that night Figt pushed them hard. She seemed distant and angry. Moralin found herself wondering again about what was happening at the village. What were the survivors eating now? Was Ooden well? She tried asking Figt questions, but the other girl answered only in short bursts. No, they had never before captured a skulkuk. No, they had never had this kind of disaster.

"Does thee ever wonder about . . . back there?"

Figt only answered with a mocking question. "Does this Kadu worry about walking by the moon's light?"

Moralin glanced up. The moon's eye was almost open. This must be—she counted—the fifth or sixth time since her capture. Sometimes she still longed for warm, comforting blackness. But there were whole nights where she hardly noticed. Could a person get used to anything? "My name is Moralin" was all she said.

Figt glared with warrior eyes and stalked ahead.

They slept a few hours, but at dawn Figt shook her awake, indicating that they should walk. She kept looking around with uneasy glances. Moralin couldn't help glancing around, too. Soon hot dust thickened the air. Moralin scratched at the insect bites and sand on her arms. The plant designs had disappeared.

Finally Figt pointed with her chin. Moralin squinted. A small bluff? When they reached it, they crawled up, slipping in the sand until they could grab on to bushes at the top. Figt whispered into the beastie's ear, and it squirmed silently through the bushes.

Moralin imitated the beastie. Her legs scraped the ground. When Figt plucked a small leaf from the bush and chewed on it, she did, too. The leaf had hardly any moisture and left her mouth feeling drier than ever. Figt raised herself to her hands and knees.

"Ssssst." Figt made the soft, hushing sound between her teeth. She eased herself through the bushes almost without noise. Moralin followed until Figt hesitated, putting one hand on the beastie, which leaned against her. For a while the three of them lay motionless.

Moralin heard nothing except a soft whirring sound and the rustle of a slight breeze in the bushes. Then the sound of a human voice blew toward them. Figt eased forward—and stopped. Moralin wiggled up beside her and peered over.

Short, squat men, perhaps twenty of them, with powerful-looking arms were making a slow circle on the plain below them. They were wearing only loin-cloths. Moralin tried to make out the faces. They had deformed noses. No. Their noses were pierced. Each nose had a yellow stick or bone jutting out from either side. A streak of brown paint ran from the top of each man's forehead, down his nose. The men carried curved knives made of some kind of metal.

The beastie gave a low growl. "Mud-ugly," Moralin whispered in Delagua. "Doing what?" she added in Arkera.

Figt said nothing.

After a while the circle shifted, and Moralin saw that they had surrounded a garrag. It swung its massive head. Several of the men leaped forward to wedge a stick in the animal's jaws. The garrag clamped down. Shouts echoed as the men tightened in a coil. A few moments later they scattered. They had used the stick to flip the garrag onto its back, where its powerful legs rowed helplessly.

She watched the men stab the animal. Without ceremony, they carried it off. Moralin turned. Figt had an ill and stricken look on her face. And why not? Praise the Great Ones that the men had a garrag to focus on. "How can thee make . . ." She paused and started over, this time using a Delagua word. "How can thee make *revenge* on such as that?" The other girl curled in the sand and moaned.

By now heat had seized the day, and they stayed on the bluff in the slight shade of the bushes. At dusk Moralin opened her eyes and saw that Figt was sitting up, gazing at nothing. "What is it?"

"Strawhopper eaters." Figt spit in the grass. "They also want to eat garrag and other unclean things." She put her head down on her arm.

"They are the sand dwellers . . . the ones who killed thy family?"

"Yes." The whisper shimmered in the air as if it were

something alive. "I made those who survived tell me everything. They said these strawhopper eaters cut the leg of Nazet, my baby brother." Figt pointed to the curved scar by her ankle. "So I cut my own leg." With one finger, she made the gesture of a tear, showing her mourning. "If only I had gone with them."

"Shall we walk?" Moralin asked after a while.

"No." Figt's voice was harsh and final.

This was the end of their journey then. They both would die here in some kind of attempt at revenge. Moralin whispered the death prayer and sat in silence. Did the messengers for judgment and pity venture into the sand waste?

As night wore on, she watched the way the moon shadows folded themselves over rocks and bushes, turning everything strange, and she longed for swallowing darkness. She offered Figt a few last berries from her pouch, and Figt held out a precious piece of dried meat in return.

After a while Moralin half slept, her fingers twined in the beastie's fur.

In the early morning Figt found a fleshy fruit covered with spines and showed Moralin how to scrape off the prickles and suck out the juices. As they ate, Moralin suddenly wished she could tell the other girl that she herself sometimes wondered about that terrible day she'd been dangled over the wall. If she hadn't run away from Mother and Grandmother after that fish, would the rough hands have grabbed her? Such small things could change a whole life—a decision not to go with family one day. A fish.

Her thoughts hissed and burned as if some legless creeper had been let loose in her head. If not for the fish, she might have grown up small and sweet, loving the leap of the thread rather than the leap and spin of bodies. The thud of the heddle rather than the thud of a body hitting the ground. She might have become wonderfully skilled at cloth work, and when it came her time to enter the secret temple chambers— Figt bumped her arm, interrupting her thoughts.

For a moment they were looking boldly at each

other. Moralin wondered if her own face was anything like Figt's, full of desperation and despair. "What can thee do against them?" she asked. "Forget them." She made her voice soft and coaxing. "Why should you and I not find a way out of this sand place?"

The huge, colorless sky stretched above them was so vast she thought she could drown in it. Figt appeared to be thinking. "Where would we go?"

"I will try to find the city. As for thee—" She tried to think if there was any place the girl could hide until the rains came.

"All right," Figt finally said with no emotion. "But give thy word. Help me get inside thy city."

"Inside?" In Delagua she said, "What craziness is this?"

"Give it." Figt grabbed Moralin's arm roughly.

"But—"

She spoke in a tumble of words. "Here is my story. The strawhopper eaters sold my brother and sister to the Delagua. My sister escaped and reached the camp in the forest."

"No one escapes from the city," Moralin said firmly.

Figt gave her a baleful look. "Thee did." She rushed on. "My sister died in the night from the wounds of her journey. I have decided I will go to my brother."

A distant shout made them both fall silent. In a few quick moments they crossed the bluff. Sand blew up in Moralin's face. She could feel grit between her teeth. In a low voice she said, "Thee cannot call what happened to me—"

"Ssst."

Figt crept to the edge. She gave a tiny grunt. Moralin wriggled to see. Below were the people who had captured the garrag the day before, whooping and running in a place where coarse, dried grass poked through the sand.

She lay beside Figt on her stomach to watch. "What are they doing?"

"Catching strawhoppers."

"Ugh. Too close." Moralin scooted and then crawled backward. Figt started to follow, but with a whooshing noise, the ground under her broke. She let out a short, scared burst of sound and disappeared.

The beastie barked. "Back." Moralin grabbed for him. "And shut up." She hugged him around the neck and held on.

CHAPTER

SEVENTEEN

MORALIN LAY SALT-STILL AND BURIED HER head in the beastie's fur. The beastie smelled of sweat and dust, but it was alive and the nearest thing she had to an ally in this place. "Oh, Cora Linga," she whispered. "How I wish you could hear me." Please don't let the strawhopper eaters look up here. I'll forgive this beastie and take care of it. I'll do anything.

Don't be rock-stupid. These people apparently were allies of the Delagua. But she felt ill, thinking of their pierced noses and menacing faces.

They were shouting, "Hai, hai." Their whoops echoed in the silence and then dissolved.

"We're going to be all right," Moralin whispered into the beastie's ear.

Behind her on the bluff, the bushes rustled. "Hai!"

Moralin whirled. A man was running toward her. The painted bone quivered in his nose, and he had black teeth. She scrambled frantically for anything—a rock, a stick—and then he leaped onto her. She let herself go limp and felt his heavy body relax slightly. Then, with a quick twist, she was out from under him and on her feet. Another man tossed a net over the beastie, which growled and snapped. Three more approached and others behind them. In a moment, Moralin, too, was tangled in a net, swinging in the air. She squealed and struggled.

Shhhh-shhhh. Calm. Be strong. The sun glinted off the sand as the men began to trot.

She turned her breathing from rapids to a meandering river. Horrible though these people were, she might not die in the hands of strawhopper eaters if she could let them know she was Delagua. Since they had metal knives, some of them must be traders.

Delagua soldiers never came this far from home anymore. But what if she could make these people believe someone was coming to rescue her? Maybe such barbarians even knew the way to the city. Maybe they were her salvation.

She imagined herself kneeling at the foot of Cora Linga's altar to give thanks. Now Lan was running from the house to leap into her arms. And then? Better not to think beyond the altar and the house.

The men halted, talking in low, ominous murmurs. She twisted to see. A man stuck a reed into the sand and slurped noisily. If Old Tamlin were here, he'd find some way to ask questions, to get the lore and desert wisdom of these strawhopper eaters. She could almost feel the water on her cracked tongue, but when they were finished, they picked her up and rushed on.

Once she thought she heard the beastie whimper, and she wiggled and squirmed, trying to see it, until someone hit her. Eventually she could tell they were climbing a hill. A thick smell of meat made her stomach grumble. The men stopped and dumped her out.

She was in the middle of a camp even more uncivilized than that of the Arkera. These strawhopper eaters lived in upside-down bird nests. Moralin saw a skinny child crawl out of one. Wearing only a string of small bones around its waist, it ran off, squealing.

Just beyond the houses, strange humped animals were tethered. They stared ahead with haughty expressions and chewed. Their faces said they would gladly bite the arm of anyone who came near.

Where was Figt? Ah. Standing, tied, at the side of the camp. She had her eyes closed, and her face was wax and salt. "My father's body, my mother's body," she had said. Perhaps Figt would be glad to die in a place where her parents had died.

Three men grabbed Moralin and looped rope around her wrists and ankles. "I am Delagua," she said loudly, but no one seemed to understand. She watched them secure the beastie in its net, squat around a gourd, and begin to scoop food into their mouths. A group of giggling children surrounded Moralin. One poked her arm. The others laughed.

A woman walked over and stood leaning on a polished walking stick, watching Moralin thoughtfully, chewing on something. Moralin kept her face impassive. The woman did not wear a bone through her nose, but her hair stood out in stiff clay-red spikes. She called to two women who appeared to be grinding grain.

The women put down their grinding stones and sauntered over. They wore strands of seeds and bones around their necks and waists. "I am Delagua," Moralin said loudly. She knew this was probably babble to them. They made hissing sounds as they watched her. Moralin raised her tied wrists and thumped her chest. "Delagua." Very slowly. She pointed with her chin at Figt. "Arkera."

"Delagua . . . Delagua . . ." Now they seemed to catch the word. Other women pushed and shoved to see her. In a few moments men's faces, too, gaped at her.

"Delagua," she said again, making her mouth broad and wide. The group stood murmuring, watching her. One of the men growled a short word.

"Uh-uh-uh." The first woman's earrings clinked as she bobbed her head. She pointed and muttered.

Now they all must pinch her skin, stroke her hair. Moralin itched to slap their fingers. They ran back and forth between Figt and her. She could tell from their gestures they saw no difference. It made her want to scream.

One by one, the eating men left their food and wandered over to lean calmly on polished sticks. What did she have to show them she was Delagua? The Arkera had taken everything.

The first woman said something, gesturing with her walking stick. In a flash, Moralin grabbed for it with both hands. "Hai!" the woman shouted, leaping back. Putting on her most pleading face, Moralin argued, moving her hands as well as she could, that if they would just untie her, give her the stick, she would show them.

"Come on." She coaxed in Delagua. "What can I do against all of you? You don't have any other entertainment out here. At least I can give you something to watch before you kill me."

One of the children imitated Moralin's tone. Everyone laughed. Then a man used his teeth to loosen the knots in the ropes, and the woman gave Moralin her stick.

They formed a circle around her, curved knives out. All right. Shake off the ropes. Step to the right, turn to the left, one knee on the sand. She touched her forehead. Lunge, retreat. Arms ready. Begin. She swung the stick this way and that, fighting an imaginary opponent.

A whispering started that became almost a chant. She heard "Delagua" several times and hoped they were saying it would be dangerous to kill a Delagua. "Soldiers are coming for me." She acted out the marching, made a fierce face.

One man shrugged. What was he saying?

The others murmured agreement.

The man used his fingers to indicate a person walking out into the sand. His fingers showed her falling. Writhing. Lying still. Everyone laughed again.

"Fine. I'll die there. Give me the beastie." Moralin pointed to show what she wanted.

The people in the circle looked at one another. No one seemed to care. A child ran to loosen the beastie from the net. Moralin picked it up, heavy as it was, and staggered out of the circle and away from the camp.

She couldn't walk far with the beastie wriggling to get down. Anyway, the sun was withering hot, and why should she hurry? They had let her go. To die in the sand. She sat down in the shade of a prickly bush and put her arms around the beastie's neck, holding it tightly. It nudged at her arm with its nose and whined.

"I know," Moralin told it. "But how could I have saved her?"

The beastie looked at her with a mournful expression and thumped its tail on the ground.

It was mud-ugly to remember those curved knives

and how Figt might die. "If it makes thee feel any better," she said, "we are going to die, too." She patted the beastie absently, thinking about what Figt had said about her family. Moralin's own father was someone she had never seen except distantly on ceremony days. She could recite facts about him, as about any royal-born, but she had never spoken to him.

With the sun grinding into her face, she held the beastie with one arm and used her other hand to empty the contents of her pouch on the ground. Arkera herbs. The blue bead, which glittered and winked. Figt had been the one to find food. Moralin nudged the things this way and that. A few women in the circle had been wearing beads, but they were small and nowhere as lovely as this one.

The beastie looked at Moralin with dark, unblinking eyes.

"Maybe I'll find someone else to help me," she told it. She closed her eyes, trying to turn her thoughts to wonderful, empty blackness.

The beastie whined again. "All right." Moralin was

suddenly scooping things into the pouch. "All right. Let's go get Figt."

The beastie scrambled to its feet and barked. "Are you giving in to weakness?" Old Tamlin would say. "The Delagua are strong because they show no mercy to their enemies."

"No, the girl was useful to me," Moralin said aloud, turning toward the camp. "I will die out here in the waste without her."

The beastie barked, and Moralin was struck with sharp panic that it was too late. But when she hurried back over the top of the hill, Figt had slumped to the ground. Now women and children were gathered around the food.

Moralin strode into the camp as a Delagua should: noble, proud, the way Grandmother could walk into a room and have everyone look, just because she had entered. "Hear me."

She didn't want to guess what their expressions meant. "Delagua." She went on loudly. "I am Delagua."

A woman said something to the others, her mouth full. Others muttered agreement.

Moralin looked for the man who had told her she could go and pointed to Figt. "That one comes with me." She motioned to try to make him understand. "I want her, too."

A woman made a rough gesture and said a word. Moralin could easily guess its meaning. No.

A babble of words followed.

Moralin stepped forward, waiting, the way Grandmother would do it. When they all were looking, she stuck out her hand and opened her fingers. The bead glinted on her palm.

She couldn't have asked for a better response. A man shouted, "Hai!" and jumped back. Others crowded closer. Nodding and mumbling, they gaped at the bead. Someone reached out, but she quickly closed her palm.

"Give me"—Moralin pointed—"the girl. I will give you"—she held it up—"the bead." She closed her fist and put her hand behind her back. She walked a short distance and waited. Let them decide how much they wanted it. She hoped they were remembering the soldiers. Hoped they wouldn't think it was worth the danger of killing a Delagua for the bead.

As they talked, she patted the beastie. *Calm.* What had Cora Linga said about the bead that night in the Arkera camp? "Beware, beware of her. Use her not, the daughter of the sky." But it was the only thing she had.

"I wonder if any human being has ever defied the Great Ones and won," she said softly to the beastie. "Maybe I'll be struck dead—maybe by the hands of these strawhopper eaters." Her voice cracked. "For my disobedience."

The beastie rubbed its head against her hand.

As she watched, two men cuffed each other. Someone else whacked one of the men with a stick. Two women, their voices hard with anger, joined in. She waited, motionless, until they beckoned to her. A tall woman stuck out her palm.

Moralin kept her voice calm. "Wait. Give us food." It was easy to act out eating.

One of the men stepped over to the gourd and handed it to her. It was almost empty. Someone else walked over to Figt and worked the rope off. Moralin gave the bead to the woman, who smoothed it lovingly against her palm.

"Hai!" the others said, crowding around.

"Hurry," Moralin told Figt. Only when they had walked far from the camp did she stop and sniff the gourd.

Figt scuffed her feet in the sand. "One thing I cannot understand," she mumbled, "who would eat this thing?" She said nothing more and would not touch the food.

Moralin shrugged. As she ate, she did her best to explain that she had decided she would take Figt to the city. What could it hurt? If Figt did somehow manage to get in and out alive, she would discover Delagua secrets were well hidden. "I give you my word," she said.

Figt only grunted.

Stung, Moralin curled her fingers to keep from

slapping the other girl. Was she supposed to understand someone who did not say thank you and whose face was expressionless as the sand? She felt proud of her Delagua training that would force her to keep her word even when it meant being honorable to someone who wronged her.

Naturally, this brother wouldn't be alive. Prisoners were brought as tribute into the city. They were killed during the great ceremonies. But maybe seeing his place of death would give Figt some kind of peace.

Moralin would even try to get Figt out alive again. This she would do because the other girl was helping her find her way through the sand waste. And because she had given her word.

CHAPTER

EIGHTEEN

THE LONGER THEY WALKED, THE MORE Moralin saw the strawhopper eaters were right. Someone would stumble over their bones in the sand.

She scolded herself bitterly. Her last link to Cora Linga, the bead, was now gone, and for what? To save an Arkera. Even if she did get close enough for Cora Linga to hear her prayers again, she had proved herself unworthy. She tried to picture Lan running toward her but saw only Ooden's face.

Figt showed her that they could suck slimy, hot juice from the plants that stabbed their feet. They took turns letting the beastie lick slime from their fingers. When they crawled against some rocks for a little shade, they found a tiny pool of water trapped there. Moralin held her drops on her tongue as long as possible. "Any idea where we are?"

Figt wearily held up three fingers. What did that mean? Three what? Moralin opened her mouth, but no words came out.

In front of her, something moved in the grass. A strawhopper. She slowly stretched out her arm. Got it. Quickly, before she could think, she put it in her mouth and bit down. It crunched between her teeth and tasted slightly of salt and sand. "Come on," she said to Figt.

Figt shook her head with horror. But in the end they both had no choice. Even the beastie ate strawhoppers.

They survived by crawling from one patch of coarse grass to another. "The strawhopper eaters spoke truth," Moralin croaked in a hoarse whisper one evening.

"We are strawhopper eaters," Figt said, and

Moralin's cracked lips stretched into a grim smile. "But look. If we could reach that place . . ."

Moralin peered at the faint outline of something rising out of the horizon.

All that night they dragged on, lifting feet that had turned to iron. When they could not walk anymore, they crawled. The beastie licked their faces, but with a dry tongue. When morning came, the rise looked no closer.

Moralin stopped, full of despair. She pulled herself to her feet and fumbled in her pouch. Maybe some herb could dull the pain. How good even Arkera food would taste. Or a strawhopper—even that. She looked up at the fading half-moon, daring it to swallow her. "Figt." She had to force the word out of her dry, scratchy throat. "Know anything that can save us?"

The other girl said nothing. Moralin could see in her eyes that she, too, was giving up.

"I'm going to keep going," Moralin whispered. Just then her foot caught on a root, and she was too tired to catch herself as she fell. *May I stand with courage and look death in the eye.* But she lay without moving.

CHAPTER

NINETEEN

HANDS PULLED AT HER. SHE WAS FLOATING. Her spirit was clearly leaving her body. When would she face the judgment messengers?

Something huge loomed, and she opened her mouth to scream, but her breath turned into a wind that bounced bits of sand across the scorched flatland. In her dream she was so dry that her tongue scraped against the roof of her mouth. Her fingertips rubbed together, gritty and cold. Her bones had turned to powder and were slowly crumbling. Of course. She had died unworthy. But the Great Ones were merciful, and she dreamed of water poured into her mouth.

The nightmare turned to a dream haze of blacks and browns that glowed around her. She did nothing for a long time except soak up colors. Then she felt she was falling, and when she put her hands out to catch herself, they touched cloth. She opened her eyes.

The sweet, smoky scent of burning oil was strong, but she was in the dark. She groped until she felt her pouch and waterskin beside her. Grandmother said a great man's treasures were buried with him for the journey to the land of the afterdead. Perhaps she had brought hers along, too.

"Ah." Though the voice was soft, Moralin recoiled. Were there tests she could pass here in the afterworld and become worthy again?

"Who are you?" she said loudly. "Friend or enemy of the Delagua?"

"We ally with everyone and no one." It was a female spirit that spoke Delagua words with a slight accent.

Moralin's head ached. Was this a guard, watching over her until the judgment messengers could come?

The voice spoke again. "We are those who walk bravely." Had the spirit come nearer? Moralin tensed, ready to defend herself. "We aid anyone and fight no one."

If they didn't fight, perhaps she could overpower this guard. But as she tried to lift her arm, it was a rock. She sank back into sleep.

For a while she thought the music was part of her dream. The flute notes sounded like someone crying, then someone dancing. Gradually she knew she was awake. Had she reached the end of her journey to the afterworld? She opened her eyes, hoping to see dawn-golden ripples of light, hoping to see Cora Linga's merciful face. Or at least a stern messenger. What she saw was the laughter-filled eyes of the song maker.

"So you did die," she whispered. Good. Wherever she was, he would be a welcome guide.

"I'm not dead."

What? She tried to sit up, and he reached out to help. She was all gnawing hunger. It was the hunger that convinced her she was alive. He lifted water to her lips, and she drowned herself in its thick, cool wetness. He put bread into her hands.

It was the best thing she had ever eaten. She chewed every sweet crumb, and he gave her more.

"Scouts found you on our borders. Why did you go into the sand waste? How did you manage to leave deep mother?" He didn't wait for an answer but rushed on. "Do you know that you are now only four days' walk from the Delagua city?" He studied her face. "That doesn't frighten you, does it?"

She couldn't find the words for how she felt. But frightened? That didn't make sense. She looked at him. He was sitting in a pool of sunshine.

"Here." He put something into her hands. Some kind of fruit? He laughed as she sniffed it. "Yes, to eat."

She bit into it eagerly. It reminded her of all the fruits and sweet-tasting flowers that had ever delighted her mouth. They were in a cave but not a dark and dank one like the cave where the Arkera gathered salt. It was not small like the one where they had crouched to escape the garrag. The walls were a warm reddish color, and sunlight streamed from a hole high above her head. "I was afraid the Arkera had killed you."

"You still call them by that name? It means 'snake,' you know." He gave her a close look. "They revere snakes, but they do not want to be called snakes."

"You said, 'I half expect I'll feel a spear sliding between my shoulder blades as I leave.'"

"They did give me a scolding for getting talkative with a prisoner. One of the warriors sent me on my way with a good shove." He grinned. "But they also gave me extra salt for the two days when I translated for you. The reward for my season's work of translating was the first I brought to my people." She saw a familiar pride flick in his eyes.

Her head wobbled. Stay alert, she told herself, but it felt so good to sink back, to shut her eyes.

∽

A sound of barking came from far away. She sat up on the mattress and looked around for the beastie, but apparently it had been a guest only in her dream. "Hello?" she called out hopefully.

Song-maker was quickly kneeling at her side. His hands cupped a bowl of red clay, thin and delicate, with leaf patterns painted along the rim. He helped her drink. Sweet goat's milk.

She wanted to say thank you, but awkwardness kept the words back. "Where are—"

"Your friends? They, too, slept and slept. Now they are practicing walking again. Ready to try?"

He helped her up. She took an unsteady step forward, grimacing at the pain of unused muscles and at the word "friends." The clothes she was wearing were made of soft white cloth and reminded her of the tunic and pants from the fighting yard.

"This is the smoothest way." He guided her out the mouth of the cave and onto a small terrace of stubby grass.

A baby goat looked up, green clumps hanging from

its mouth, and shouted *maaaaa*, running to its mother. Moralin and Song-maker laughed.

He helped her over the terrace wall and down to a path that ran along a gulch between high, misshapen walls. This place looked as if the Great Ones had played here long ago, molding the soft rock into weird shapes, swishing the red with streaks of white and deep scarlet. Over there they had mounded the clay to look like a wildcat's paw. A few steps ahead, swirls and lines made a strange pattern, some Great One's gleeful giant painting.

She was so intrigued that she forgot to feel her stiffness. After a bit the walls widened, and high above them the sun smeared the rocks with orange. Soon they passed a fissure cloaked in shadow. It looked like an ominous secret passageway, but at the far end she caught a glimpse of a building carved right out of the rock. Someone had painted rust-colored goats that ran on spindly legs over its pillars.

How did Song-maker know her language so well? The Delagua city must not be as completely closed as those in power insisted. She wondered if one of her people had sought refuge here and become a teacher.

Song-maker left the main path and led her through a small passageway that wiggled and finally dipped toward a wide, oval mouth. They walked into the tunnel. In the dim light she saw a painted herd of animals with flapping ears and thin legs. "Get ready," he said.

She frowned. Ready for what?

When they stepped out, the green—after so many days of yellow and red—made her eyes water. If she looked up at the cliffs, she saw nothing but reds and oranges and browns, but at their feet lay a bowl of green with a blue pool cupped at the bottom. A spring must bubble under these rocks. The sides of the bowl had been carved into terraces, planted with hundreds of trees and bushes.

"This is where my mother and brothers work." Song-maker's voice was proud. He helped her down narrow steps shaped out of the soft rock.

"So many plants." She paused by a small tree. Something about the smell reminded her of home, and she felt a powerful longing rise in her throat.

"My mother's father cultivated this garden. At the cave mouth where travelers unpacked and shook out dirt, he noticed that strange plants sprouted. He started to inspect each bundle."

"Why sift dirt for something so tiny?"

Song-maker hesitated. His face turned grave. "Because the Arkera and Delagua both forced us to bring them tribute. Always food and animals. In bad years . . . our own young."

He had used the snake name, she noticed.

"Our backs groaned with work, but we still starved as we carried our food to others." He paused and then burst out, "What could we do? If we stopped giving what they demanded, we knew our enemies would leap on us and tear us to pieces. People huddled in their caves and thought of nothing except the terror that might strike if the crops failed or sand trapped our roaming animals."

She didn't know what to say. Tribute always came to the strong. It was the way of the world. "What about fighting back?" she finally managed to ask.

"Some argued for that. My mother's father proposed another way." Song-maker dropped to his knees. "What if we had things only we knew how to grow? Things the powerful would want?" His fingers brushed a plant. "These roots, for instance, turned out to produce yellow dye that pleases The People. Using such things we have been slowly tipping the scale from tribute to trade, especially with the Arkera."

A shout made them look back to the cave opening. A young boy hopped down the steps and gave something to Song-maker. Moralin stared with curiosity at the lines and pointed marks on the thin bark.

He turned and started back up the stairs. "Enough talk. Your friends are back."

What kind of magic had told him this? She hurried after him, eager to ask. But his mood seemed to have turned dark. He didn't stop until they had gotten back to the room where she had left her things. "Wait here."

Glad for the rest, she sank down on the mattress. It

was filled with sweet-smelling straw, and she curled into it. So . . . soft . . .

Wetness woke her up. A river of wetness. A slopping, warm tongue. She put her arms around the beastie's neck and pulled herself back to a sitting position.

Figt stood looking down at her. "Kadu? You are well?"

Moralin stretched her arms over her head. Her feelings were as tangled as thread.

"We survived the sand waste." She had never heard Figt's voice this way, bursting with amazement. "Now the city is only four days from here. Get up. Let's go."

"How great is my joy," Moralin said. She was excited. Wasn't she? "Since we are close," she added, "it will not hurt to wait a bit longer. A few days."

She tried to ignore the puzzled, pained look on Figt's face. There was no reason for the other girl to be so eager, she told herself hotly. She went on, "We have need for great caution and careful planning. I gave my word, but there are many dangers in the Delagua city besides me."

Figt drew herself up. "I am one of The People. I am prepared to die."

"Yes. Well . . ." A bit sheepish, astonished at her own desire to stay, Moralin chewed her lip. Song-maker had much he could show her. Of course once she was home, all other wonders would be nothing.

Figt was quiet for a while. Then she said, "I think thee has forgotten that dangers are here, too. My people talk of places that draw strangers in and they never want to get home."

Moralin tensed. How could she have stopped thinking clearly? She thought of Song-maker's dark mood and the way he'd said, "We have been slowly tipping the scale from tribute to trade." Prisoners were something to be given in tribute. Some prisoners could even be used in trade. She scrambled to her feet and scooped up her things.

Figt looked at her with approval. "Hurry. Maybe they won't expect us to try to escape so soon." The beastie made three circles around Moralin, barking.

Figt moved to the door and looked out. "No guards

that I can see," she said. "Can thee walk?"

"I'm fine. Does thee have thy knife?"

"The strawhopper eaters took it. I have my blow-pipe." Figt pointed to an opening at the back of the cave. Moralin followed her through the low door, and they were in a corridor lit by candles. But they had walked for only a little way when the ground became slick and hard. The beastie slipped and scrambled, trying to keep its balance. The click of its toenails was the only sound.

"How do thee know this is the right way?" Moralin whispered.

Figt paused. "I—I thought it was."

"Look." Moralin pointed with amazement to baskets, heaped with green fruit.

Figt gave her tunic a tug. "My people tell stories of people trapped forever in strange places because they tasted the food."

Grandmother had told such a story, too. And Moralin had already eaten. Frightened now, she started to run. Above the sound of her footsteps, a weird singing rose. She put her fingers in her ears. Maybe they also used music to lure people into wanting to stay.

The tunnel twisted. As Moralin dashed around the corner, she saw an opening ahead. She slowed, gasping. Figt pushed past her.

"Wait." Moralin grabbed for the back of Figt's tunic. They were too late. She remembered the look on Song-maker's face as he told her of the years of tribute. Remembered how he could make bark and black paint speak. He must have let the guards know they were escaping. One now blocked the gate.

CHAPTER TWENTY

"WE ONLY WANT TO REACH THE OUTSIDE world so we can go home," Figt called.

The guard replied calmly. "Those who walk bravely say the whole world is ever anybody's home."

"May we go then?"

Moralin could feel the fight rising in her shoulders. In her mind's eye, she saw the guard pulling out a knife, leaping toward them. To her astonishment he simply stepped to one side.

A few minutes later they were standing on the coarse grass in front of the cave. From the smell of the air Moralin could tell it had rained today. Dry season must be over. A path led off to the right. Why was she hesitating, feeling a strange heart clench of loss when her heart should be full of joy and relief?

"Look." Figt held out a piece of the thin bark with black lines on it. "A map. Song-maker also gave me food and other supplies."

"But why, then—"

Figt walked away. "Come on," she called back, her voice commanding.

Moralin followed, dark resentment swelling. Careful. She loosened the fists out of her hands.

The path wandered calmly through the strange and twisted rock formations she had glimpsed when she and Song-maker were on their way to the place of the spring. She could spot openings in the cliff face. They were framed with carvings, and black goats grazed on the small aprons of land.

Luckily she and Figt saw no one. Once, though, they heard a child whimper. Two voices, one male, one female, hushed it. Did both mothers and fathers live with children in these caves then? How strange.

Even when there were no more dwellings, the smell of fruit and some kind of tart vegetable floated from gardens that must be hidden nearby. Here thin waterfalls spilled over the cliff face.

Figt studied the map. "Easy to become lost."

Moralin said nothing.

After a while Figt took out bread and fruit, which she ate greedily and shared with the beastie. She offered some to Moralin, who refused.

The beastie ran from side to side, sniffing at roots of occasional bushes and once digging frantically in a hole where a small animal was probably hiding. It didn't stop until Figt whistled. Then it bounded after them.

Moralin seethed as she walked. Why had Figt tricked her into thinking of the cave people as enemies? Why should an Arkera be so ready to walk to her death in the Delagua city? Did she think entering with a highborn would give her some protection? What would the other girl say if she knew the Great Ones were angry with Moralin and would be sure to doom this journey? In fact probably the nearer they got to the temple, the more danger there would be.

The thought made her forget Figt and think about her own worries. Was there any way to regain favor with Cora Linga? The Great Ones help those who use their own strength. She made a silent vow. From now on she would use only her own strength.

Four days, Song-maker had said. How long until she saw something she recognized—perhaps one of the sacred hills? It was odd to try to imagine herself truly back home. Her awa clan would already have been in the temple service for a long time by now. Well, if she could just make amends with Cora Linga, something would work out. She was Old Tamlin's granddaughter.

Calmly she tried to make her plans. Later, if they ran into patrolling soldiers, what story could she say? The first step must be to try to find the jamara tree. Then?

In the afternoon, walking under stone-gray clouds, they clambered over lumpy foothills and found themselves free of the red rocks. Far away Moralin saw a mountain with smoke drifting out of its head. "The people say skulkuks once lived there," Figt said. "Ancient eggs can still be found in the caves, so old their shells have turned to rocks."

A wondrous idea. The breeze fluttered the cloth of Moralin's tunic. For one wild moment she thought that instead of going to the Delagua city, they could turn aside and find one of these rock eggs. What was wrong with her? Soon you will see your family, she thought, scolding herself. Yes, seeing her family was all that mattered.

"Now the skulkuks live in that other place of broken trees." Figt had put on her expressionless warrior voice. She pulled two white cloaks out of her bag and gave one to Moralin.

"Why did your people try such a dangerous thing?" Moralin settled the cloak around her shoulders. Was she shivering from the chill in the air or from the memories of the village in flames? Could she ever pay a trader or someone to find out what had happened to Ooden?

Figt didn't answer. Ahead, the path branched. She took out the map. "Why take that creature, I mean," Moralin insisted. The wind caught Figt's cloak, making it float. "That was rock-stupid."

Figt faced her. Her cheek twitched. "Any danger was worth the chance to get inside the Delagua city. Because of what thy people do to mine."

"And thy people?" Moralin's voice rose. The wind gave a sudden soft groan. "Thee did not see my friends killed and left by the path. All people do these things."

"The cave people seem honorable," Figt said stubbornly.

Thunder grumbled softly. Dark clouds were crawling toward them. The sky looked just the way Moralin felt inside. "Thee lied to me." Now Moralin's voice was trembling. "They had given thee things for our journey."

"I saw thy eyes." The other girl spit the words at her. "I was not going to come so close to my brother only to have thee lose heart."

Moralin flushed. Figt might just as well have straight out called her a coward. Before she could stop herself, she grabbed the map and ripped it in two.

Figt gaped at her.

Moralin was instantly full of fire-hot shame. How could she endanger their trip this close to home? "I'm sorry." She held out the two pieces. But as Figt reached for them, the wind caught one and whirled it away. Moralin leaped. It skittered a few steps ahead. A patter of rain thumped wet fingers on the path, flicking up dust. Moralin caught the bark. As she handed it to Figt, she saw the black paint on her hand.

They took shelter under a tree. At least the cloak was warm, Moralin thought, slumping under it. "So, what does thee really know about these cave people?" she asked Figt finally.

"My mother told me a little." Her voice was not

angry anymore, but sad. "I like to think of the way her eyes looked as she spoke of them."

"Does thee remember her face?" Moralin flushed, wishing the words back inside her mouth.

Figt looked at her. "You don't need to say 'thee' to me if you are going to ask this question."

"I thought 'you' was . . ." She tried to think of the word for "impolite."

"Yes." Figt scooped up a stick. She threw it hard, and the beastie bounced off into the rain. "But close friends also use it with each other." For a while she was silent. Then she said, "My mother was not born one of The People. She was taken in as you were."

In bad years, Song-maker had said. *Our own young.* "Perhaps she grew up in those caves."

"Yes," Figt said thoughtfully. "Her voice was the sound of water. I kept remembering her while we were there."

Moralin thought of her own elegant mother. What would she say when she saw her rumpled daughter?

"After she died," Figt went on, her voice tight with

pain, "I was given to my aunts, but I ran from them many times. I was happy to begin training to be a warrior. Until . . ."

The wet beastie ran up with a small creature in its mouth. "This mighty hunter," Figt said softly. Her eyes glistened.

Moralin waggled her hand, palm down, in understanding. There was nothing to say, but the gesture hung there between them until Figt looked away.

Eventually, Figt began to play the gourd she carried. Moralin reached out, and Figt let her try it. Seeing that Moralin couldn't coax any sound at all from it, Figt finally smiled a little.

When the rain stopped, they stepped out. Moralin pointed toward what looked like a city of dark stones. "I think this is the way."

Figt hesitated.

"I'm sure." Moralin was surprised by the firmness of her voice.

Soon rocks stood on either side of them like giant,

impassive people. Moralin was about to say that perhaps they should turn around, but before she got the words out, Figt gestured to one of the rocks. A whistling sound rose from a small hole in it. The beastie growled and sniffed.

At the bottom of the slope, something glistened as if a piece of sky had slipped out of place. Moralin imagined giant sky fish flapping around, breaking a hole for the sky to soak through.

What did she know of the lands around the city? A swift river lay to the east, but people could not use it for water in dry season because . . . she felt dizzy, remembering.

Grandmother had told this story only once. Servant girls had clutched one another. Moralin had wrapped her arms around her legs and, full of delicious fear, stared up at Grandmother. "People kept getting killed by rocks. Was it the way these rocks were formed?" Grandmother had asked, not waiting for an answer. "Or did monstrous animals sleep under the rocks? Animals that shifted their weight and grumbled a warning when footsteps disturbed their sleep?"

Figt pulled the blowpipe from her pack. Another whistling rose in the rocks. "Let's go back." Moralin turned and saw a rock sliding toward them slowly, the way sand slid down a dune. The beastie snarled.

"Run," Moralin shouted. What could a blowpipe do?

Figt and the beastie bounded down the path. Moralin dashed after them. Here the water sounded like a legless creeper rustling in the bushes. Behind her she thought she heard the mutter of something waking up. Ahead a fallen tree stretched across the river. Figt reached the trunk, scooped the beastie up, and ran across on agile feet.

A rock rumbled by and splashed into the river, showering Moralin with drops. "Hurry," Figt shouted. Panting, Moralin scrambled onto the wet tree and took five unsteady steps. Behind her, a blow made the tree shake. She grabbed a bare branch, trying not to think about the snarling water below.

A second rock hit. Moralin stood salt-still, feeling the log shudder. The beastie barked wildly from the other end, and Moralin turned to look behind her. A huge rock was rolling down the hill. She forced herself to move, running with little sideways steps. In the moment she leaped off, she felt the jolt and heard a giant cracking sound. The two pieces of the broken trunk slipped slowly into the river, where the swift current dragged them away.

She fumbled her way up the bank on legs of twisted string. Dark was falling quickly, and she could barely make out a grassy knoll. To the left, rocks formed a sheltered spot, but she didn't want to be anywhere near rocks tonight. She flopped down, put her arms around the beastie, and pulled it close. After she could talk again, she whispered, "You hero," in its ear.

"The People say this river is guarded by a monster," Figt said. "I thought it was a tale. Lucky we are that it is only the start of the little rains. And for the tree."

Moralin was glad the other girl said nothing about being lost, even though it was obvious they were.

CHAPTER

TWENTY-ONE

WHEN THE FIRST LIGHT TOUCHED HER EYELIDS, Moralin rolled over. The beastie licked her face and wiggled to its feet. She crawled up the knoll and looked around. Then she buried her head in the beastie's fur.

Behind them the river gurgled and hissed like some unfriendly creature. Ahead was a high, sheer cliff. This piece of land where she and Figt had slept was cradled between the river and the cliff. They could drink from the river, unless the water was bad. But they would have no food.

Back at the bottom of the knoll, she clutched her cloak and pulled sleep around her. This time she dreamed of terrible things: figures reaching milk-white fingers for her, stones crashing toward her head. She woke up moaning.

Grandmother had always said that Moralin would bring trouble onto herself if she didn't learn to control her anger. Now she had. Worse yet, Figt was right; she had not wanted to leave the caves. Why?

Since she was a child, people said, "You have Delagua blood and courage and wisdom and strength." Always Delagua. Mother would use herself as an example. As a highborn married to a royalborn, she almost never saw her husband, who had his own duties and responsibilities. She lived patiently in his mother's house, far from her own family. Did even shadows ever complain about all their work? The Delagua were the most noble and wise.

She remembered Song-maker's words as he knelt by

the plant of yellow dye. What if there was another way to be strong? What if . . .

No. She shoved the wicked thoughts away and took out a piece of fruit, bit into it, and listened to the way her teeth squeaked on the skin. Better enjoy the sweet juice blooming in her mouth. This food in their pouches was the last they would ever eat.

After a while Figt rolled over, stood, and climbed the knoll. Moralin braced herself for a scream of anger. But Figt just sat up there and played notes on her little gourd. The beastie ran around, stopping to roll back and forth in the dirt.

"Cora Linga," Moralin whispered, "are you close enough to hear me? I have been so unworthy." Nothing answered except a slight wind ruffling the river.

She was staring blankly, smoothing the beastie's fur, when Figt came back. "My plan is ready."

Moralin felt silver hope spring in her. It quickly died. What could help them now?

"I see I can make a way up the cliff." Figt motioned,

and they climbed the knoll and stood looking at the frowning rock face. "The People have long known the ways of climbing."

"Ooden told me."

"And it is true." Figt wrapped her cloak around her waist and tied it.

Moralin shook her head.

"You did it once."

"That cliff was not as tall as this one. There were holes for my hands and feet." And I hadn't yet disobeyed and angered Cora Linga, she added silently.

Figt sat down and took off her sandals. She turned them thoughtfully in her hands. "But not impossible."

"For me, impossible."

Figt looked at her with curiosity.

Moralin fought the shame that pooled in her chest. Why speak of this? Maybe Figt would have pity and stay. Let the three of them die here together on the ground. Ah. She hung her head. Song-maker was right. They were her friends.

"This is my story," she said. For the first time in her

life, using words and gestures, she did her best to show what it was like to be scooped up and hauled, wiggling and screaming, down the stone streets, up the wall. "Someone . . . held me out over the wall. I think it was a woman. She was going to drop me." Moralin choked and stopped.

"But you were a child then." Figt's voice was matter-of-fact. "You must do this now and get home." Figt tied her sandals together with a leather thong, humming.

Moralin tossed a small stone toward the water. Why was Figt so hard-hearted? She thought about Mamita sitting at the loom, singing as she wove the starbright threads. Would her own mother recognize her now? With her arms and legs strong and burned by the sun, her hair wild and matted?

She forced herself to study the cliff. Just doing that much made her sick. "No," she said. "I can't."

Warrior-calm, Figt reached for Moralin's sandals.

"I also know the Great Ones want us—me anyway—to fail."

Figt tied the sandals around her waist beside the cloak. "This cliff says I may climb." After a moment she added, "You gave me my life." Though she didn't say the words, Moralin knew what she meant. "I can save yours."

Moralin looked at her with scorn and frustration. "What about the beastie? It's going to climb, too?"

Figt rubbed the beastie's ears. "It stays. A beastie can't come into the Delagua city." She stooped and picked up a small rock. "If I live, I will come back. If not, perhaps another tree will fall across the river. If all fails, this beastie and I will at least share death."

"That's stupid," Moralin said. "Without me, how will you even get into the Delagua city?"

Figt began to hum again.

"What if you do get in? You think your brother is just going to be there? Standing inside the gates? You don't know anything of the Delagua city."

Figt only gave her a wry smile. "This is why I need you." She walked to the cliff, tested several spots with her fingers, and then calmly began to scrape with the rock. When she had hollowed out a little hole, she reached higher and began to scrape again. "Follow me," she called. But she didn't turn to see if Moralin would.

As Moralin watched in horror, Figt maneuvered herself upward, finding handholds that turned into foot holes. She almost seemed to have a picture of the cliff face in her mind, moving confidently to the left or right, grasping at things too small for Moralin to see. Looking higher, Moralin realized Figt must be aiming at a tiny tree that grew near the top, far above them between the rocks. The beastie watched, too. Once it whined and wagged its tail. Figt didn't respond.

Moralin sat down and crossed her arms over her chest, thinking about the words of the Delagua death prayer. She closed her eyes. Better to starve than fall, tumbling over and over in the air, waiting helplessly for the ground's deathblow.

"It can be done." Moralin jumped. Figt had returned on silent feet and was squatting beside her.

"I'm sure. You must help. Remember your word."

So. Did it all come to duty after all? It must be her fate to die falling, crashing to the ground where her bones would break to little pieces. "You know," she said slowly, "I don't know how to find your brother."

"No?" Figt sounded uneasy for the first time. "He must be what you called a shadow."

Moralin started. "That's not right."

"It's true." Figt gave her a rough shake. "You will see. When my sister came to me, she was wearing one of those white masks."

Moralin sat without moving. She could feel her body turning to sand. The shadows were not . . . simple as children? They were not given masks as a kindness for their grotesque faces? A river of unreasoned anger tumbled her in its rapids, pounding her head on its rocks. At Figt for shaking her arm and for this terrible information. At the girls who had mocked her all her life and then had lured her outside the city gates, only to desert her by dying so quickly. At Salla for giving up. And at the cruelty of whoever had held her

dangling over the wall, laughing. And at her own sick-stomach helpless, terrible fear.

"Come on." Figt stepped to the cliff and began to climb again.

The beastie whined softly. Figt had left food in a pile. Most beasties would have gobbled up that pile of food, but this one seemed to know it shouldn't.

Moralin bent down to rub its soft fur. "Anyway," she told it, "if Figt never comes back for you, maybe you could get across the river someday. You're so brave, a brave, brave beastie."

The beastie licked her hand.

Moralin dropped to her knees and hugged it. "Good-bye." She put her face into its back and breathed that musty, warm smell. "You turned out to be a friend after all."

She walked off quickly. Mustn't cry and make the task even more impossible.

Figt had reached a ledge and was clinging there. It made Moralin ill to see her. "I'm coming," Moralin called. Figt gave no sign she had heard.

Make the river of fear harden. Climb on top.

She put her hand into the first hole. But she couldn't make herself move. *Shhhhh. Shhhhh.* You're all right. Go on. She imagined Old Tamlin there beside her. They were finally going to climb the city wall. If she could only go up this terrible mountain, she would see him again, Old Tamlin, the most kind and noble being who ever lived.

TWENTY-TWO

CURLING HER FINGERS OVER PEBBLE-SIZE bumps, clinging with her fingertips, she crept upward, shifting her weight carefully. The pull on her fingers was agonizing. She didn't dare consider how weak her arms and fingers would be by the time she was high on the cliff.

For a few minutes she made steady progress. She had not guessed she would be strong enough to pull herself from handhold to handhold, but as if from a distance, she could see her arms moving, knew that she now had the same strong muscle she had been amazed to see in Figt that first day.

Figt called something she couldn't make out. In a few minutes Moralin saw it: a crack in the cliff face wide enough to grip with both hands. Straining, she lifted herself onto a small shelf. It stuck out only the width of her feet, but above it, the cliff sloped back a bit, so that by pressing her chest tightly into the rock, she could cautiously let her hands drop to her side and give her trembling arms a rest. She tried not to know that she was already so high she would be crippled or killed if she tumbled off.

Over and over, when Old Tamlin was trying to urge her to climb, he told her, "If you give in to your fear that you will fall, then you will indeed fall because of the fear." Was she strong enough to will herself not to give in to deathly fear? She had done it the night she walked on the coals.

At least she was relying on her own strength.

Up and up, now working the cracks that ran along

the cliff. Her toes ached. Don't picture yourself flattened and frightened. Stay away from all thoughts of the ground beneath you. Up and up.

This was so much harder than the other climb, when she had been fleeing captivity and following those who had worn the holes deep. Where was Figt? Had she reached the top? Had she fallen? The Delagua felt safe having this steep cliff—and the deep river and probably a monster beast—as protection for the city. Must let someone know it could be climbed.

After a while a wind began to whine. Moralin felt cold terror rise. Must not look up. Must not look down. Perhaps she was close enough to the temple for Cora Linga to hear her now. "Can you forgive me for wasting the bead?" she whispered. "How long it's been since I heard your voice."

Amazing she was still alive and hadn't been conquered by the garrag, the great sand waste, the monster under the rocks. She gripped harder. With or without the Great Ones, she could survive.

Suddenly her foot slipped. She was scrabbling

against the rock, her fingers clinging with strength she didn't know she had. Her frantic foot found the toe-hold again. But now her mouth was dry, and she couldn't catch her breath.

"Forgive me," she choked out. I'm a fly, about to be brushed off this cliff.

Nothing.

Her heart seemed to be rising out of her chest with the panic. Her head was light and dizzy. She concentrated all her will and eased upward, one more step. As she slid her chest and stomach along the rock, she must have crushed a small plant growing there, because the smell, a dust-musky odor of herbs, filled her head. And in that intense moment, she felt something she had never felt, a presence beyond even the Great Ones, something impossible to name.

The presence surrounded her and filled her, and she could keep going. Up and up. Up and up. Her hand touched a root. The tree? Was she already that high? Yes. With every last bit of strength in her shaking arms and legs, she dragged herself up and wrapped both arms around the thin tree. She could move no farther.

The rock was cold against her cheek. Her arms trembled violently. How long could they hold before she let go and flew off? She saw herself falling through the air, a drop of water shaken from the fur of some huge being, falling, falling. Terror hammered her chest.

"Are you there?" She felt as if she were shouting the words aloud to the presence around her, though she was probably only whispering. "I want to hear your voice before I die."

As if in answer, the wind increased. For a moment or two it whistled and sighed, but the voice of the presence was not in the wind.

Then the wind was gone. The air—or was it her own head?—was filled with a rumbling, but the voice of the presence was not in the rumbling.

As the sound disappeared, all that was left was still silence. And in the silence Moralin heard a kind of voice. She couldn't make out any words, but her whole body was filled with singing. Yes, this was a holy place. She was ready to die now. She could hear the breeze sweeping across the summit a little way above her. It knocked off small stones that clattered down on her head and hands.

"Moralin?" It was Figt. A little way above. Her voice almost too thin to be real.

Moralin clung to the tree and didn't try to answer. Her arms felt swollen and cramped. Close by, an evening bird flitted out from its cliff nest with a whir of wings.

"Moralin." Her name a second time. Her real name. "Hold on."

Her arms were on fire. She would have to let go. She looked down to the rocks below to see what she was going to hit.

Figt said her name again, softly this time. Moralin felt, rather than saw, the other girl beside her. "I'm going to tie your cloak around you and knot it to mine," Figt said. "Climb with me. Move when I say."

"I can't." She listened to the gasp of her words and, for a few long moments, her own panting.

"There. It's like a rope now, holding you." Figt pried one of Moralin's hands from the tree.

"The cloth will break."

"Move when I tell you to. The People know everything about climbing."

Moralin felt the cave people's cloth, tight around her waist. Shaking, she reached for a handhold and eased forward.

"Almost at the top," Figt called after it seemed that great gulps of time had passed. Hand. Toe. Up. But she had no strength to hoist herself over. She felt Figt's hands on her arms. For one awful moment she was dangling in empty space, and then she was being hauled like a great fish out of the ocean of emptiness to lie gasping at the edge of the cliff.

The sun was high in the turquoise sky as Moralin curled like a baby, clutching her trembling legs. Figt disappeared. Returned. "I can't stand up," Moralin whispered.

"I want you to climb the hill," Figt said in a voice urgent with excitement or maybe fear. "You will be amazed."

She wouldn't be amazed. She could almost smell the city. Home.

CHAPTER
TWENTY-THREE

W HILE SHE WAITED FOR HER LEGS TO STOP quivering, they made plans. "We should rest in that grove of trees." Moralin pointed. "We have the cave people's clothes, which should help unless a soldier tries to speak to us."

Finally she felt strong enough to climb with Figt holding on to her arm. For a long time she stood at the top of the hill, looking at the vague outlines of the city. She knew it was farther than it looked in the sharp, dry air. Don't weep, she told herself. You're almost home.

Figt was gazing out to the north. "What's that?"

Moralin shielded her eyes. In grayish green foothills, something glinted: a tiny speck. "Maybe it's where the caravans come from. They bring resin and golden plates. Even birds that talk. They trade these and other things for cloth."

"I should want to see a place of talking birds and gold."

Moralin sighed. She would, too.

Figt gripped her arm as if she thought Moralin might tumble down the slope if she let go. They moved to the grove to make plans and wait out the afternoon rain. After they used the last of the healing oils from the helicht plant on their scratches and scrapes, they huddled together under their cloaks. Moralin lay still, listening to the rain fleck against the leaves, looking at their four hands on the cloth.

She felt filled with reverence for skin, for breathing. Were there other sacred places in the world where the holy presence was strong? Would she ever feel it again?

Wasn't it strange how you could see the most wonder-ful things in the world, but if your heart wasn't open to wonder, everything looked no better than mud?

She fell asleep and dreamed that Cora Linga came to her. For once the Great One didn't speak in riddles but said, "You did well, my child."

"Cora Linga," she cried. "Nothing happened as you said it would."

"Hardly anything happens as humans think it will." Cora Linga looked like her picture on the tapestry in the temple, only with light shining everywhere around and inside her.

"I thought I was supposed to use my own strength, but Figt had to save me on the cliff. And you told me not to use the blue bead."

"Your strength will always include the people around you and even animals." Cora Linga looked deeply into Moralin's eyes. "As for the bead, calamity comes to those who use such things selfishly."

"But—But what will happen to me?"

Cora Linga bent over and touched Moralin's forehead.

"On the night when the invisible ones walk, ah, then is the spider's web torn. Ah, then does the fly escape."

Moralin felt a cool stinging on her forehead. "I had almost everything wrong," she whispered.

"Humans often do." Cora Linga's form faded and disappeared.

Moralin woke to feel Figt trembling beside her. She reached over to shake the other girl awake, but before she touched her, Figt said, "I'm not asleep." Her voice was ghostly. "I'm—I'm afraid. Why did I think I could go into such a city?"

Moralin let her hand settle on Figt's arm. She had been wrong. Figt might be an uncivilized Arkera, but she was honorable and courageous. Not knowing what else to do, she simply echoed what Figt had said by the cliff. "It can be done." If only she was sure it could be.

To calm themselves, they took stock, spreading out the cloaks and dumping out their pouches. As well as she could, Moralin explained where they were now and where they needed to go. "I hope we can travel unseen if we wait for dark."

She poked at some crumbled herbs with her finger, thinking about Cora Linga's riddle. After a while she hesitantly tried to tell the dream to Figt. "Know what it might mean?"

Figt was using her teeth to sharpen a stick. "At first when I was forced to become a solitary, I had to search everywhere for food." She spit out a piece of bark. "As I wandered, this same one appeared and showed me a vision of a great hall."

"Cora Linga? Oh, I don't think so."

"We call her Amma Tamu. She comes to us in her toad form. She says the Delagua are always putting toads in trap boxes."

Moralin chewed her thumbnail, shocked into silence.

"Shall I describe the vision? Maybe it will help."

Moralin nodded weakly. "Maybe."

"A flying insect came to me and touched me with its feelers. Its wings were white and black. I saw it lay hundreds of eggs and then die." Figt's voice was dream-calm. In front of her eyes, the eggs turned into wiggling worms. Girls ran back and forth bringing leaves. All the worms, as one, swiveled their heads in a strange dance. Liquid spewed out of their mouths and turned into delicate threads that the worms wrapped and wrapped around their bodies. They slept for three days and turned from worms into . . . Figt hesitated. "A small pouch that could be held in a person's hand."

The worms had to be symbols for something. In the old stories, things often happened in threes. Moralin noticed that she had bitten one of her fingernails down to the skin. She curled her fingers against her sweaty palm.

"I saw a girl standing before a roaring fire." Figt went on. "She threw the worms into the fire. The worms died from the heat, but their pouches did not burn. That's all." She studied Moralin's face. "Know what it means?"

Without meaning to, Moralin was chewing on another fingernail.

Figt talked on as if she would never stop. "My sister crawled into the camp too near death to talk. I gave her water, I held her hand. I was sure I could keep her from dying. She clutched something like the pouch I saw in my dream. And her mask had a strange design on it." She bent over and scratched with the stick, but the wet dirt oozed closed.

"When we're in a safe place," Moralin said, "you can take paint and show me."

Most of the afternoon Figt couldn't seem to stop pacing. She wanted to leave the grove, but Moralin convinced her they should wait. "Better not to have light if we run into someone." What would her family think the first time they saw her in the light? Moralin could almost feel her mother's hand reaching out to try to fix her tangled hair.

When the sun finally landed on the horizon, flinging up ribbons of color, they stepped out from the trees. Strange feelings rumbled inside Moralin. No time to sort them out. Better to be walking. Better to plan. "From now on watch me and do what I do," she told Figt.

"Think I could pass for Delagua?"

Moralin studied her skeptically. "We'll use velees so people can't see our faces. I have clothes stored at Old

Tamlin's house. Don't walk so bold, though."

About halfway through this night a fingernail moon would rise. A moon-dark night would be best. Cora Linga, she complained silently. Why don't the Great Ones ever seem to give human beings what would be *best*?

She and Figt had told each other they would move silently, but as they walked along the base of the hill, they fell to nervous, low talk. Shadows lived in groups of twenty around the city, Moralin explained. Each of those houses had two fighters assigned to do morning, afternoon, and night inspections. Any shadow found out of place was usually struck down on the spot.

After Moralin was sure they both were prepared— and both scared—Figt said, "So I will likely die in your city. And you? What is your path?"

What indeed? How to explain the awa clan and temple service? "We, too, have initiation ceremonies" was all she could think to say.

"The path will be given then?"

Moralin replied softly, using Delagua words when

she didn't have Arkera ones, wondering how much Figt understood. After the temple service some girls became priestesses. They lived in a convent near the temple and tended the gardens. Every twenty-five days, on the first moon-dark night, they walked the streets of the city. "They do the work of the dead," she explained.

"Only this work? Forever?"

"Only this work. And no one may look upon them." She stopped, thinking. "Maybe their lives are not so terrible. It is said the convent gardens are full of fountains, trees, and fruit-sweet flowers cascading over the walls, and the priestesses eat on dishes of gold, as do the royalborn."

She remembered the glint she and Figt had seen far in the distance. What was it like, this birthplace of the gold? "If a girl is royalborn and marries a royalborn"— she went on—"she lives in a grand house on an island in the middle of the lake, hidden from the eyes of common people. Others marry common men. I don't know what dishes they use."

She had always thought she would marry well

because she was royalborn through her father's blood. Once when Mother was angry about Moralin's awkward weaving, she said Moralin might go into the convent because she was neither beautiful nor particularly skilled. But she'd always hoped Mother had been speaking only from anger.

The grass caught in her sandals as they walked hesitantly under the squinting eye of the moon. A tree loomed, scaring Moralin for a moment, its branches reaching out like thick arms. "Let's wait here until it's light enough for me to find the place," she whispered.

On the hard ground she tried to sleep, but her storm-wild thoughts ran in circles, snakes chasing their tails. What if someone had locked the door at the end of the tunnel? No, Old Tamlin would have figured out that she had gone that way, and he would make sure it was still open. But what terrible fate waited for a Delagua caught bringing an Arkera inside the city? They were two worms crawling into a feverbird's nest.

Dawn melted the darkness and wove a morning sky of moon-pale, cool cloth. They ate the last of the food, then cautiously climbed the hill. When they reached the top, Moralin couldn't move. She felt blasted open with hunger and joy.

If she could only show Figt everything about the city—her city. The fighting yard where she had grown strong and bold. The market with its green and purple and golden fruits, with spices spilling out of their bags and sheena peppers and many-colored grains. The stone streets. The shining yellow temple.

She made herself study the landscape. "Yes, the Great Ones have smiled on us," she whispered. In the growing light she recognized the outline of the jamara tree. As they hurried down toward it, she could smell her own fear. She glanced around for a branch she could use as a fighting stick and then realized it would be too hard to carry it with her through the hole. "Give me the sharp stick," she whispered. "Let me enter first. Come if I call."

She parted the bushes as silently as she could and squeezed through the opening. Yes! Everything was just as she had left it. She didn't see the soldier until he stepped swiftly out of the darkness, fighting stick ready.

CHAPTER
TWENTY-FOUR

HER SKIN KNEW WHAT TO DO. BEFORE SHE had time to think, she ducked and kicked, knocking her opponent's stick to the ground. She was on him in a flash, the sharp stick to his throat. His mouth opened and closed: a fish mouth, breathing water.

"Odd." His voice came out in a dry rasp. "Odd if I should be killed by the very person for whom I guard this door."

"How do you know who I am?" She made her voice tough and bold.

"Who would know these Delagua fighting moves? The granddaughter Old Tamlin set me here to watch for."

She eased so he could speak more easily, careful in case he tried to twist under her and throw her to the ground. Instead he gazed up with a strange expression. "Such a man I would serve whether he was alive or dead. And you. When I was young, I often heard him tell of the vision the Great Ones gave him when you were born: that you would someday save the city."

Now she was the one who must look like a fish.

"After the great revolt"—the man wheezed on—"he never spoke of it openly again. Some forgot. I never did."

The great revolt?

"He told us how he trained you in the fighting yard. Oh, don't look like that. He had to tell us because he knew you would come in fiercely." He closed his eyes.

"You may kill me. I would be honored to be killed by such as you."

"I've never killed anyone." She climbed off. "I'm not going to kill you."

She and Figt did tie him up with the cloaks, however, and leave him in the dark cave. A new guard would come to relieve him tomorrow afternoon, he told them. Moralin saw from marks on the cave wall that each guard worked for five days. As they lowered themselves through the trapdoor, he called after them, "I'm so sorry. A great man."

"What did he say?" Figt asked.

"I don't know." She showed Figt where to put her hand and went as quickly as she dared.

He told us how he trained you. Now everyone would know for sure she was a freak. Old Tamlin would have sworn them to secrecy, of course, but such secrets never held.

Almost there. Fear was harsh in her throat. Keep going. She fumbled for the lamp and tinder purse and then knelt. Once, twice, three times, she struck sharply down, watching the tiny red-hot flakes as they fell onto the piece of flax. When it flared, she lit the lamp with quick fingers. She pushed oh-so-gently on the door, but it didn't budge. Had someone fastened the bolt on the other side? She shoved, and the door flew open.

A moment later they were inside the house. Figt made a small, nervous noise. Moralin knelt and kissed the floor. *He told us how he trained you.* Nothing mattered except that she was home.

"Smell that?" Figt's voice floated eerily in the dim lamplight.

Moralin breathed in frankincense and scent of tree sap.

"This smell speaks to me," Figt whispered. "Someone in this house—" She looked small and afraid.

"Stay here." Moralin rushed down the hall, up the stairs. As she stepped inside the room, she saw Old Tamlin, a silent heap on the bed.

"No." She wanted to howl, but the word came out

as a whimper. So much she had needed to ask him, but death had crunched him in its jaws, stronger than any garrag's. Her eyes stung. She had waited and longed to pour out her adventures to him. Who else would understand or even listen?

"Old Tamlin," she said softly. "You showed me so many things. Help me understand. This city . . . the shadows . . ." She moaned. Shadows were not like children. They were like wood animals, trapped in a reed cage, like a skulkuk crashing against the bars. The fever-bird was not protecting the worm; it was crushing it.

Old Tamlin had known all this. Dazed, she moved to the bed. His skin shone with resin and wax. He must have died a few days ago, but no one would enter this room until the priestesses came. She looked boldly into his face for the first time, blinking away the tears, and touched his cheek, something she never would have done while he towered over her.

Smells of cinnamon and wax and myrrh rose from his body. Was his spirit here, being judged by the messengers of the Great Ones? Her throat burned with sorrow, but she knew she must not interfere with his efforts to show the Great Ones that he had been worthy. She hoped they were seeing a stern man look gently at the blistered palm of a little girl. "Thank you for everything you gave me." She covered her mouth with her hands and hurried away.

Figt still crouched in the hall with the sharp stick and blowpipe ready. "It's all right," Moralin told her sadly. The shadows would be gone; a fighter would have come for them when Old Tamlin became ill. Now even those who had loved and served Old Tamlin would not dare come near.

But had she and Figt not survived the place of Arkera death and spent the night with human bones? Had she not lived under the hollow eye of the moon? She refused to be afraid in this Delagua house.

Full of melancholy memories, she led Figt across the house to the room Old Tamlin had always kept for her. Nothing had been touched. She gathered an armful of silky Delagua cloth, remembering Old Tamlin's voice: "The cloth saves us, Moralin. It's the only way."

She turned. Figt's gaze was fixed on a sword fastened to the wall. With a sound of disgust, she dropped the stick on the floor.

Moralin handed a dress to the other girl. "Put this on. No, no, this way." She stepped back. "You look funny as a Delagua."

Figt curled her shoulders uncomfortably. "You slept here? So closed off from air?"

"Not here. I kept things for when I visited Old Tamlin. But this place was almost . . ." She paused and looked around. "Home." She choked on the word and couldn't go on.

The first dress she tried ripped. She dropped it on the floor and found a bigger one. Then she rummaged in an ivory pot for the paint and brushes she had used to make pictures when she was a child.

Figt took them. The brush whispered softly against the floor. Moralin bent to watch. The skin on her fingertips hurt, and she told herself not to chew her nails again, but she did anyway.

A one-legged bird. She walked around to study the design from another direction. "These marks show where the shadows live."

Figt's eyes were shiny with hope.

"But . . ." Moralin shook her head. "I've never seen this one before."

CHAPTER TWENTY-FIVE

MORALIN TRIED NOT TO LOOK AT THE OTHER
girl's disappointed face. "I can think of only one place
where we might find a clue," she said slowly. The
shadows lived in small groups around the city. But in
one room, shadows mingled for a short time. Old
Tamlin had been in charge of it.

With Old Tamlin's death, perhaps the place would
be in some confusion. If she and Figt could find a
shadow with the one-legged bird on his mask, they

might be able to figure out a way to question him.

She told Figt her idea, not bothering to say that failure would end in death for both of them. That was true even if they did nothing. Together they climbed the steps. Several times Figt stumbled and muttered.

"So," Moralin said, "the mighty Arkera warrior woman is stopped by a Delagua dress." By the time they reached the top, though, she said, "These clothes are unhandy when you're out of practice."

She led Figt to a long window cut out of the wall that allowed them to see the outside steps. A breeze brushed her face as she peeked out. When the sun reached the second step, Old Tamlin always began his duties. Once he had heaped forbidden on forbidden and taken her along. *He said you would someday save the city.*

In Old Tamlin's chamber they put the netting over their faces, wrapped themselves in the cloaks, and pulled up the hoods. One of Old Tamlin's men usually guarded this secret entrance, but now it was deserted.

Moralin slid the bolt, and they entered the fighting yard. Walk boldly. Manage your fear.

Fighting sticks swished and cracked. Someone yelped in pain. She had thought she would never see this place again. They strode past a group of gossiping soldiers. Through another door. Down some stairs. Old Tamlin had done this every morning. "If a commander stops us," she had told Figt, "he will question us and kill us. But any underling will think we were sent to do Old Tamlin's work."

At the bottom they turned left into a long, dim hallway hung with tapestries that showed Delagua history. From these the fighters learned, proud to take their place in some future tapestry. Moralin made her way cautiously toward the first small pool of light, cast by a high window. Silver-gray shapes seemed to rustle, but when Moralin whirled around, her heart lurching, no person stepped forward to challenge them.

The shushing of their cloaks sounded loud in the hallway. Figt made a startled noise as hers caught around her ankles. From the tapestry on the wall, Cora

Linga's eyes gazed down with a strange expression. Amusement? Pity?

The next tapestry made Moralin bite her lip and taste blood. Delagua victory, Arkera defeat. Shocking things were being done to the Arkera people in the picture. The soldiers had looked majestic, almost holy, when she had walked here with Old Tamlin. Now they looked fierce. She might have even said bloodthirsty and cruel. Some were guarding shadows who tended fires. Bright pieces of Delagua cloth danced. *The cloth is the only way.*

She moved on to a tapestry with five panels. First, sacred visitors stood before a Delagua royalborn. Then the visitors offered a precious jewel that had a hole in its middle. The weaver of the third panel had used vivid colors to show the Delagua ruler beckoning to a worm. In the next panel the worm was crawling into the jewel, trailing a thin silken line. Last, the gem hung on the silken string around the ruler's neck, while the worm was lifted high on a golden tray and all the people stood around with open mouths, giving the joy cry.

Keep going. Would the tapestry she needed be here? Yes. She stopped in front of the weaving she most wanted—and did not want—to see. Shadows ran through the streets with guards after them. A few were outside the gate. On top of the wall a shadow dangled a screaming child. So this was the great revolt. The child—

A thump somewhere above them nudged Moralin out of her thoughts. They hurried the remaining steps to the end of the corridor, and she put her hand to the door. A cry shuddered, deep inside. Please, Cora Linga. She pushed the door open.

The room stank with a sour smell of sweat and old food. A shadow knelt in front of a soldier, who had turned toward the sound of the door. Moralin made her voice into a low growl. "Shadow inspection." To her relief, he merely nodded.

Shadows sat along the walls or stretched on mats. This was the room for those who had committed some transgression or whose lives changed when calamity forced adjustments to a household. Old

Tamlin had come here every morning and afternoon.

Please, Cora Linga. We have come so far. May we find some clue here. She and Figt walked up and down the lines. "Look up. Look up." No. No one had the mark of the one-legged bird.

Back in Old Tamlin's house, Figt gave a bitter laugh. "We can never find him."

"It's not good." Moralin's spirit was stone. How could it be that sometimes people came so far and did so much, still only to fail? While Figt curled in a corner, Moralin sat, lost in her tangled thoughts about the history she had seen.

When the Delagua chose to retreat inside the city walls, they demanded tribute from nearby settlements but they were also given the sacred secret of cloth making so they could trade for other things they wanted. Who would keep the sacred secrets? Even shadows couldn't be trusted with that.

She shook herself loose of her musings. They must seek the temple, she decided, and beg Cora Linga's help. "Come over here," she told Figt. "Let me put your velee on."

Figt stood still while Moralin covered both of their heads. "Do the best you can," she said, her words slightly muffled by the cloth. "We need our faces hidden."

As she opened Old Tamlin's little-used back door, she strained against the velee, wishing she could see more clearly. Everything seemed both sweetly familiar and dazzlingly new. It was as if she had lived here a long time ago. At first she had to look around after every few steps. Water was starting to run in the channels again, and its voice murmured secrets to her, but she didn't know its language. She tripped as one thing and then another caught her attention. Finally Figt made an impatient, anguished sound, and they began to walk more quickly through the bustling city.

There. That was the temple wall where she had seen Salla and the others. Poor Salla.

They climbed. Moralin touched her forehead, and they stepped inside. The great hall was filled with sunlight. She went to the central tapestry and lifted her arms. "Help us, Cora Linga."

Silence. She thought about the other tapestries she had just seen. At least she now knew the answer to the question she had asked herself for so long. It wasn't a fish that changed her life. No, the guard said that before the great revolt Old Tamlin spoke often of his vision. That was why the shadows wanted her dead. Some shadow had probably also risked death to tell the fierce trainer that she was a girl. The shadows wouldn't have forgotten, any more than the guard at the trapdoor had.

She studied the toad scene. *Speak to me, Cora Linga.* She moved on to one where the Great Ones were shown as spiders. "I'm here. I'm waiting. Show me how to find the shadow we seek." She barely breathed the words, as softly as if she could keep even the other Great Ones from hearing.

But though she felt dizzy with the effort of listening, she heard nothing. Nothing except the whoosh and shush of her own blood in her ears.

She must at least get Figt out of here tonight, while she still had a way to reach the secret tunnel. Even now the messengers for judgment and pity must be wrestling with Old Tamlin's spirit, making their decision. Tomorrow, after the priestesses had come for his body, the house would belong to Old Tamlin no longer.

She saw the tapestry that had scared her so much when she was a child. In the first panel, priestesses in their dui-duis, carrying bodies covered in white cloth, walked the silent, dark streets of the city to the temple. The next day's dawn brought temple mourning for families. Then bodies were taken to the convent for seventy days. After that, the bodies of highborn and royalborn Delagua were carried back to the temple, where they lay in an underground room with the body of a shadow on either side to serve them in death even as in life.

She returned to the first panel. "On the night when the invisible ones walk," Cora Linga had told her in the dream. "Then does the fly escape." No one dared look on the priestesses while they did their work, and tonight such would walk. Moralin nodded slowly. Could two people search a whole city in one night and find a one-legged bird? No. But what else was there to do?

When they were safely back, she explained. Tonight, the first moon-dark night, white figures would leave the temple. No one was allowed to look upon them or speak to them. So she and Figt could also walk through the city if they could only find the place where the dui-duis were kept.

"The priestesses will come to this house for your grandfather?" Figt asked.

Moralin stuttered out the word "yes" and fell silent.

Later, as they shared a piece of hard bread, Figt explained that The People said a dead person's bones must be out where the birds could pick them clean and where the sun and wind could purify them. Then their spirits would return to the air and not hover to steal people's breath.

It comforted Moralin a bit that The People, too,

thought spirits went somewhere. She held out a piece of cheese and managed a small smile when Figt wrinkled her nose at the taste. Then they stretched on the floor of the great room to rest. After a long time Moralin said, "Figt."

"Hmm?" The other girl was either full of her own pale thoughts or nearly asleep.

"Never mind." Easier not even to try to find the words.

As the feverbirds whistled, signaling their evening's hunting, Moralin stood up. "Should we wear the velee?" Figt asked.

"I don't know." Moralin rubbed the silk cloth nervously between her fingers. "My people believe it is death to look upon a priestess, so they will be in their houses. And the streets will be dark with no moon."

"We can move better without them."

In the end they decided to leave them behind. When night swallowed the sun, they left the house to walk swiftly through the streets. "Afraid?" Moralin whispered.

"Yes." Figt was silent for a moment. "Afraid?" she asked.

"Yes."

Silence cloaked the temple. Even priests and elders must not look on a priestess doing death work. Moralin hoped the stairs were in the same place as in the fighting yard. Important buildings were oriented to the stars and probably designed much the same way. Yes. And when they reached the bottom, she saw a lamplit hall to her left, just as with the fighting yard.

One thing was different: an alcove straight ahead. She motioned, and they quickly crossed the hall and stepped into it. The back wall was crisscrossed with red lines. In the center was a tapestry of a young girl kneeling. *Cora Linga. What do we do now?*

Something creaked at the end of the hall.

"If someone finds us here?" Figt asked.

Moralin silently drew one finger across her throat. As if in answer, a sword clanked against stone.

Moralin caught the gasp that leaped in her throat. *Shhhh-shhhh*. Perhaps the men were not coming this way.

She heard a drip, drip of water far away. Then . . . footsteps. Maybe three men. Walking down the corridor.

She tried to swallow, but her mouth was sand-dry. To reach the stairs, they would have to walk right in front of the approaching men. Anyplace else to hide? Anyplace at all?

No.

Once the men reached this room, she and Figt would surely be seen.

Then?

Moralin remembered the feel of her finger on her throat.

CHAPTER TWENTY-SIX

So she would die a Delagua death after all. She was suddenly glad she had gotten a chance to see amazing things. Who would have thought even Grandmother's stories could not hold the whole of the frightening and marvelous world out beyond the wall? And the voice on the cliff.

Slap, slap. Sandals on stone.

Nothing here but walls and floor. They'd be seen anywhere in this empty room. *Slap, slap.* Perhaps twenty footsteps more, and the soldiers would reach the stairs.

Help me die bravely, Cora Linga. All those times she had escaped death. Cora Linga had surely been with her the whole time after all. But now that the sword of the enemy was at her throat . . .

Wait. What had Cora Linga told her that night in the Arkera camp? "Go to the web when a sword is at your throat." But she had gone to the web in the hollow log.

Slap, slap.

No! Humans almost always got it wrong. Daughter of the night. The bloodred web. Go . . .

Slap, slap. Maybe ten more footsteps before the soldiers reached them.

Go to the web. With one quick motion, Moralin pulled Figt—rush, hush—up against the kneeling figure.

Several things happened almost at the same time. From somewhere deep, she heard chanting begin. The footsteps stopped. A man cursed. At their backs a bolt squeaked, and she felt cool air.

A door had been opened. Moralin took a deep breath and pulled Figt around the edge of the tapestry and inside.

They were in a huge, dim room that smelled of incense and smoke. A robed figure, walking away from them, was beating on a drum, singing some kind of summons.

Ah. The invisible ones would now walk. She and Figt must also become invisible. Moralin silently pointed to dui-duis draped on a web made of cloth.

In a few swift steps, she had reached them and was pulling a dui-dui hurriedly over her head. She backed into the river of white cloth, hoping Figt was following, hoping they were now hidden ripples on that river. When the drum had thrummed ten more times, she heard footsteps, saw—through the eyeholes—a woman with a shaved head reach for a dui-dui. And another. The priestesses walked solemnly, looking at the ground.

Moralin joined the stream of figures. Was Figt behind her? Soon she could see that the line was approaching the woman with the drum. Moralin mimicked the person in front and felt something pressed into her hand. She glanced down. Three pieces of cloth, painted with symbols.

They moved into a lamplit room. Around the walls were tapestries, a huge map of the city. All right. The pieces of cloth were instructions to go to certain households to collect the dead. The priestesses found their way with this map. She tested her idea, looking for Old Tamlin's house. Yes, it was marked as a coiled creeper.

She was glad for the chanting that must cover her loud and leaping heart. Study each section. North. South. East. West. Nothing. Someone touched her elbow.

She slowly turned. Figt was trying to show her something. The one-legged bird was here in the temple. Of course.

CHAPTER TWENTY-SEVEN

ALMOST ALL THE SHADOWS HAD PROBABLY worked here until the uprising had forced the Delagua to scatter them. They would be needed for the back-breaking demands of the cloth.

Watch. Listen. Do what the others do. The priest-esses seemed to work in twos and threes, taking the supplies they needed, rolled straw mats and white sheets of cloth. When she and Figt were back out in the corridor, Moralin looked around. Doors now stood open. She heard the *shiick, shiiick* of a sword being sharpened. Guards—by the stairs. One coughed. "Dusty night."

Shhh-shh-shh. Cora Linga, be with us.

"Deep dryness was bad this year." She had heard this man in the fighting yard, shouting at the boys. "The little rains haven't helped much yet."

"Many lost," the first man said. "Fortunately mostly shadows."

They laughed. Then one nudged the others and turned quickly as Moralin and Figt approached.

Down the corridor, past more guards, who hastily faced the wall. Into the room. Five rows of shadows sleeping on cots. About ten in each row. "See him?" Moralin's whisper was hoarse with the fear she was holding in. She stepped slowly and deliberately. Figt reached out and put her hand on Moralin's shoulder.

Masks. One-legged birds. Behind each mask was a face. How could the Delagua keep something with a human face in a cage, when she couldn't even bear to hold a star-footed wood creature?

The squeeze startled her. Figt gestured at the leg of the boy and traced the half-moon scar in the air. Quickly Moralin unrolled the straw mat. What if he cried out?

Figt bent over him.

"Are you death, heard my wish and come for me?" he whispered.

"Hush." Figt eased her hands under his arms. "Lie still as death."

When he was covered with the white cloth, they threaded their way out the door, down the corridor past the guards. At the top of the stairs, they found a dark spot in the temple and set down their burden.

Figt pulled another dui-dui from underneath the one she was wearing. "As I've discovered," Moralin whispered, "just wishing for death is not enough to make death come."

They retraced their steps. Moralin went first, wary until she was sure the priestesses had not yet come for Old Tamlin. Inside her childhood room they pulled off their dui-duis. Nazet made a small noise of astonishment.

"My brother." Figt picked up one of his hands and covered it with kisses,. His blank, masked face stared at her.

Later Moralin sat on the floor outside her room, hugging her knees. One time when she was young, she had been caught in a big rain, and she had raced along the stone streets, watching the ferocious, tantrum wind whirl leaves from the trees. Now she trembled as if she were once again caught by that storm.

She had known Nazet would be angry, of course, but still she was stunned by the pain and fury in his eyes. He refused to speak while she was in the room. Of course, why should he? What human being would be able to break years of such training . . . and hatred?

Eventually she had stepped into the hall, beckoning for Figt to come with her. "Can you see if he knows anything about the rooms where the girls do temple service? Tell him your dream. Anything will help."

If only she could talk to Old Tamlin just one more time. Tell him what she now knew. Ask his advice.

She moaned, letting her head droop to her knees. Her people had done this. Old Tamlin had done it.

Sometime tomorrow workers would fill this house. It would have to be cleaned and made ready for some new official. She glanced down at the painted squares they had dropped on the floor. What kind of cry would go up when bodies were discovered still in their houses and not at the temple?

She scrambled to her feet and paced fearfully, frantically, a river of steps up and down the hall, trying to think. Trying to plan. Finally Figt opened the door.

Moralin grabbed her hand, listening as Figt explained that shadows carried wood to the door of the complex where the girls did temple service. Over the years they had listened and watched and whispered to one another, sure that someday they could make use of the little things they learned.

"Tell me everything you can," Moralin said. "I need to see this place for myself." Perhaps she could make small amends.

Back to the temple then. Be a white cloud, a white tooth, the spirit of the moon itself floating to the heart of the heart of the city. She followed priestesses down the stairs and moved without hesitation through an open door.

All right. Her neck and shoulders ached, and she let out her breath in a slow *whoosh*. Here she was. The huge main room stank of smoke, and she stopped breathing for a moment, trying not to cough. Carefully she tugged at the eyeholes of her dui-dui as she turned. There were the ovens, hungry for the wood the shadows carried. Around the edges of the room girls were asleep on cots. This was her awa clan.

Don't stay here.

She moved like a wraith into the first room that branched off. When she stepped inside it, she thought for a moment the big rains had come, spattering the roof over her. Stepping closer to the trays, she realized the sound was from fat gray worms munching on leaves. Nazet said they would eat only leaves from the trees that grew in the convent garden.

Unbelievable. The smooth and lovely water-rippling cloth started with these crawling things?

She hurried on. Here fluffy white cocoons hung from twigs. Cautiously, she reached out to touch one, brushing the soft surface lightly with her fingers. According to Nazet, the girls put most of these into the ovens to kill the moths before they could crawl out and spoil the thread. Others soaked the cocoons to loosen the filaments that were then wound onto a spool.

She breathed deeply, considering the scent of the branches that stood in huge tubs of water. A sudden sound made her stiffen and stare. Two of the white-robed figures had come into the main room. They moved toward a cot and bent over the body lying there. The girl's arms flopped as they lifted her, and even from here, Moralin saw the burns. Her skin crawled with pity for this girl who would never go home. Gently she closed her fingers around the cocoon.

∾

When she returned, Figt was jagged with worry. "Be calm," Moralin told her. "You must not think of leaving until daybreak when I can get supplies."

Though it had taken them only two days to travel from the caves to the city, Figt and Nazet would not be able to go back the same way, of course. Songmaker had said four days. The cave people must use a path somewhere to the north of the city on the edge of the Great Mountains. Figt would have to find it. Impossible without food and water.

They could shelter with the cave people until the Arkera returned to camps in the red forest—and maybe longer. They would need help to remove Nazet's mask. He would need time to heal. As for Figt, was it really possible for a solitary to rejoin the village? She thought of Ooden's many comments about the ancestors and thought it unlikely.

The caves then. Later she would allow herself to feel this sadness that was tugging at her, sadness for all they would see that she never would. For now she smiled to remember the garden. The smell of the trees. The gift she would give Figt to carry would make them welcome.

She dozed and dreamed again she was running to her mother. Mother was not smiling and not frowning—just beyond Moralin's outstretched fingers. "Mamita," Moralin called out. "Mamita, wait." She jolted awake, put on a velee, and went outside.

Night was already shot through with silver. She gasped as if seeing the beautiful city for the first time. Over there was a stable where, on mornings of velvet fog, servants stood in pools of light, holding their lamps high, lingering over the gleaming sides of the animals they brushed. How many times had she gone this way, clinging to Old Tamlin's hand or sneaking back home from the fighting yard?

Ah. There was the house. She lifted her arms as if she could somehow embrace it.

Slowly the sun's eye peered over the horizon. A faint sound of chanting floated from the temple. A woman emerged from a nearby house, sobbing. A cry of mourning rippled.

Grandmother came out the door first. Then Mother. Moralin's breath stuck in her throat. By the flower bush they leaned on each other. Though their faces were hidden and they made no noise, she could see their grief in the way they stood. Lan joined them.

Moralin took a step—and then stopped. Lan had changed. Not any longer a laughing child, she carried herself stiffly and stared ahead with dark, serious eyes.

Followed by the household servants and shadows, the three of them walked out into the street. Moralin willed them to look at her. No one did. She gazed after them, pressing her fingers against the corners of her eyes to hold back the tears.

After the street was empty again, she forced herself to move. She bent to pick a yellow moralin, breathing in the smell. She could almost taste its sweet scent.

Inside the house she allowed herself one quick glance around. Scarlet and purple hangings on the walls, glittering dishes, a tray of pretty cakes. If only Figt were here. "See how different my world is from yours," she would say.

She found the bedroom that had been hers. What would her family do when she began to tell of her adventures? Mother would raise one eyebrow in horror and dismay. "Here is my story," Moralin would say. Would anyone listen?

Maybe Lan? She thought about her sister's face. In just a few years Lan would be one of the girls standing for hours, scorched and wilted, burning the wood the shadows left by the door, tending the secrets of the beautiful cloth.

She swayed for a moment, full of sorrow, unable to move, at the same time, knowing if she didn't, she would be trapped here forever. Eventually her feet found the room with the walls that were draped with starbright weavings. "Mother," she imagined saying, "I have seen the skeletons of human beings hanging in trees. I have seen the giant wings of a skulkuk." Would she dare say this: "I know what happens in the secret temple chambers"? And what about this? "The Great Ones do not favor the Delagua and care for us above other people of the earth." She laid the yellow flower gently on the woven cover of the bed.

Quickly now. She ran to the kitchen. Threaded her way between ropes of savory and sweet herbs that shadows had braided and Mother hung here to dry. Reached for whatever she could find. She rushed out of the house and ducked into an alley. Time now to remember all the back ways to Old Tamlin's house.

In the room where Moralin had once kept her things, Figt sat rubbing her brother's hair. Nazet's head leaned against her arm. The boy appeared to be asleep or in some kind of daze.

"We must go." Moralin felt the words burst out of her, exploding in droplets. Figt looked up with astonishment. Moralin stuttered on. "Yes, I—I'm coming with you."

Though she ached to, she couldn't read the expression on Figt's face.

"Am I going to go into training in the temple? Knowing what I know?" The mixed Delagua and Arkera words rushed out. "Am I to watch the shadows carry wood for the fires? Impossible. And even if I survived temple service, am I going to spend my life inside this wall now that I've seen the outside world? Now that I've seen the mountains and the forests and the true sacred places."

Figt looked down at Nazet. "Doesn't this decision want more time?" she said cautiously.

"There is no time. We have to get out." Moralin began to fashion a bag for the supplies. "Once or twice I think I knew the truth even before we reached the city. Then I became confused. Because of what the guard said about Old Tamlin. But I figured something out tonight."

She was a flood of impatience, herding them the way a mother bird might cluck her chicks along. As they approached the door to the tunnel, Figt said, "My brother says the shadows have tried many ways of escape. When they are caught . . ." Her voice trailed off, sharp with fear.

"We won't fail." Moralin looked around one last time.

"And your family?"

Moralin considered. The guard would report only to his commander. There would be good reason to keep his story secret lest fear spread in the Delagua and hope in the shadows. "My mother will question everybody. When nobody can explain it, I think she'll take the flower I left her as a message from the afterdead. I hope the message will ease her grief."

She reached for the ivory knobs. "Together we can figure out where the cave people's path might be. And while you're rescuing that beastie, you'll need someone to stay with Nazet and keep watch at the top. How do you plan to get that barking one up the cliff?"

Figt began to laugh, and after a moment Moralin laughed, too. They put their hands over their mouths to stifle the noise. With Old Tamlin's body no longer here, someone could enter this house at any time.

"We should take more cloth." Figt turned. "We're going to need it to make some kind of sling."

"All right. Hurry, though."

They didn't speak again until they were back in the dark tunnel. "Maybe we can yet explore the golden kingdom," Figt whispered, "and see a bird that talks. Or a skulkuk egg turned to rock."

"Why are you still whispering?" Moralin asked. "Afraid the rocks will hear you?" She laughed again, giddy with relief. "The cave people go to all those places," she added.

"Nazet and I . . ." Figt was suddenly serious. "We will not rest until we find a way to open this city's gates."

CHAPTER
TWENTY-EIGHT

LATE ONE AFTERNOON, AFTER THE TIME OF little rains had come and gone and the big rains were washing the land, making everything green and new, Moralin and Figt rested on the grass in the cave garden. Moralin had been teaching Figt one of the fighting yard moves, and now sweat gleamed on their arms and dried on the backs of their necks, even though evening would be cool. "I've been wanting to ask you something," Figt said. "When exactly did you decide to leave?"

"I—I'm not sure." Moralin watched a feverbird floating on the currents of the wind high above them. The mist made spiderwebs glisten in the trees. "In the secret temple complex, I thought about Old Tamlin's vision. And what Cora Linga said in my dream. That humans hardly ever got it right."

Nearby, in the soft sunlight, the beastie snorted and moved its legs in its sleep, probably chasing some small wood creature in its dreams. Nazet rubbed its ears, then turned to dip a brush in black ink again. He had been painting endlessly, it seemed, stroking peaceful scenes onto the thin red-dish pots fired in the cave people's kilns. Would the beauty be enough to heal him? Moralin watched sadly.

"Old Tamlin thought he understood what his vision meant." She paused and then continued. "But I remembered the presence on the cliff. I asked myself how saving the city might look through sacred eyes."

"And that's when you—"

"That's when I decided to take the silken pouches. I

was thinking I should give them to you. After all, Cora Linga sent you a vision of them."

She'd realized that if she could slip away with a few cocoons before they were put onto a tray and into the ovens, a moth would break out of each. Every moth would lay many eggs. With the information Nazet had gathered and Song-maker's skills, surely the cave people would figure out ways to care for the precious worms that would hatch from the eggs somehow already knowing how to spin silk.

She finished. "But when I saw Lan and stood in my old house again, I also realized how impossible it was for me to stay."

Sometimes, at the strangest moments, a person might catch a glimpse of how the Great Ones might feel about their gifts to the world, gifts that were often twisted. From talking to the cave people, she now knew that once, long ago, the flightless, blind moths had lived all over this region. A blight had killed the trees the moths needed for food. Only the isolated trees on the Delagua island had survived to be transplanted within the convent walls.

Seeds, carelessly carried in a trade bundle, nurtured by Song-maker's grandfather, had brought the trees back to this garden. Although he hadn't known what he was doing—humans rarely did—his vision had been right. The cave dwellers would become successful people of trade. Moralin was sure that the cloth they would learn to weave would be especially exquisite.

"This theft will destroy the city, not save it," Old Tamlin would have said. But he didn't know what she knew. Hoarding the cloth making kept the royalborn eating on plates of gold and kept all the Delagua trapped with their shadows and their secrets. It turned Delagua girls into prisoners. As Old Tamlin himself had said, without the cloth, the people would have to leave their city, a beautiful city but with the heart of a snarling wildcat.

A figure appeared, walking toward them through the trees. Moralin watched as Song-maker moved under a branch and pulled it low to the ground. He let go and it sprang back, scattering a shower of raindrops and leaves. He held up his arms to the sweet water, laughing. Moralin laughed, too.

"Think." Figt pointed with her chin. "The power of cocoons."

Yes. Cocoons with moths. Moths to lay eggs. Eggs to hatch into hundreds of worms. Worms that would spin more silk thread. Thread that might one day be strong enough to pull down a wall.

It was going to take years and other people's help to spread the secrets of the cloth making. Moralin sighed and then caught herself. The Great Ones would go with her wherever she wandered. She hoped Figt and the beastie and Song-maker would go, too. They were sure to see wonders she couldn't even imagine. And luckily, as the cave people often said, "The whole world is ever anybody's home."

Mark it well.